The PEASANT PRINCESS

SCOTT and AIDAN BUELING
with MICHELLE COX

Illustrations by
CHRIS TAYLOR

Published by Parrhesia Publishing and Imprint of Leadership Books, Inc. Las Vegas, NV – New York, NY

LeadershipBooks.com

ISBN: 978-1-965401-59-0 (Hardcover - Case Laminated)
978-1-951648-57-2 (Hardcover - Jacket)
978-1-965401-60-6 (Paperback)
978-1-951648-80-0 (eBook)

Parrhesia Publishing is committed to publishing works of quality and integrity. In that spirit, we are proud to offer this book to our readers. This is a work of fiction. Unless otherwise indicated, all the names, characters, businesses, places, events, and incidents in this book are either the product of the Author's imagination or used in a fictitious manner. Any resemblance to actual persons, living or dead, or actual events is purely coincidental.

Table of Contents

1

A Sad Situation

At a long-ago time of kings, queens, and castles, two young sisters shivered in their dark and chilly room. The orphanage was entirely different from what they'd known before they came to live there.

Every day had been special when their mother and father were still alive. Father called Mother his songbird because she sang all the time. Rebecca earned the name, "Little Mother" from him, because from the time she was born, she'd always been serious and responsible.

When her little sister, Abby, was born, Rebecca took her role of big sister seriously—which was a good thing, because Abby always seemed to need rescuing from where she'd climbed or gotten into something.

Rebecca remembered the time she'd found her tiny sister sitting on the table. The older sister had shouted for Mother, "Come quick! Something is wrong with Abby. Her face has turned blue!"

1

Mother had run into the room and then burst into laughter. "Nothing's wrong. Look behind her. She's been into the blueberry cobbler I made for dinner."

Home had been filled with light and joy, with wonderful aromas coming from the cookstove, and with lots of loving hugs and kisses from Mother and Father. The orphanage was the exact opposite. It was anything but home.

Nine-year-old Rebecca Faith would give everything she had to have her parents pray with her again at night. To tuck her into bed. To have their dog jump up beside her and snuggle in, giving her happy puppy-kisses on the nose. But those days were over.

Rebecca had never expected to resemble her little sister's ragged doll, but when she looked at the wrinkled, oatmeal-colored dresses the workers at the orphanage provided for them—and saw all the stains and threadbare places in the rough fabric—the comparison couldn't be denied. She missed the clothes she and Abby used to wear. Rebecca's favorite had been a pretty blue dress that Mother made for her, and Abby had always loved to wear a bright red one.

Across the room, four-year-old Abigail hugged her doll and sang a happy song. Her eyes were squeezed closed, shutting out the small, dingy room and the circumstances that had led her and her sister there.

How is Abby always so happy? wondered nine-year-old Rebecca. She looked around the room, trying and failing to think about something other than their bleak situation. Like most mornings, the sisters sat in their tiny, dusty space, just one of seventy-seven rooms in an enormous, bleak, old building.

Rebecca was too young to be so unhappy. She missed her parents terribly. Two long years had gone by since she'd seen them. The younger sister knew only what Rebecca had told her, "Father and Mother died in a horrible fire, and then a woman who claimed to be our aunt picked us up from the church and dropped us at the orphanage. I hadn't seen her before, and we haven't seen her since."

Their parents had taught them to pray before falling asleep each night. Rebecca continued the tradition, even though she was sometimes doubtful that anyone was listening. Every night Rebecca heard Abby recite the same short prayer, "God, thank you for Rebecca, and please give me another visit to see our father and mother in heaven."

Abby was talking about some dreams she'd had, but every night that prayer brought tears to Rebecca's eyes because of a secret she'd kept from Abby since their parents died. It was a secret she didn't know if she could, or would, ever tell her sister, but the guilt tied her stomach in knots whenever she thought about it.

Most every morning, Abby woke up disappointed from not having a heavenly dream about their parents. But the few times she did get to see them in her dreams kept her reciting the prayer each night.

One morning, Abby recounted a dream about how their mother and father suddenly arrived at the orphanage to take them home. She said the family of four all hugged and laughed until their stomachs hurt—but this time, the stomach pain wasn't from the horrible orphanage food.

Rebecca closed her eyes, and in her mind, she could almost hear her parents' laughter from the years before the fire had changed their lives. Those had been such good days. Now the memories of their times together were fading, and as the years went by, she sometimes had trouble remembering what their parents' faces had looked like.

But then another memory came to Rebecca's heart. She and Father had been checking the plants in their garden, and he'd said, "Sweet girl, as you get older, you'll find that there will be good days, and there will be bad days. Remember that when the bad days come, taking your burdens to Jesus will always make things better."

More than anything, Rebecca wished she could remember what Father had said about how to do that. She'd like to ask someone, but there was nobody at the orphanage who seemed like they knew anything about God.

Perhaps God wouldn't be upset if Rebecca tried to talk to him. "I'm just a little girl, and I can't remember what Father told me about talking to you, but if you hear me, would you mind sending someone to care about me and Abby?"

Rebecca was lonely. Although the sisters loved each other, they had no friends in the dreary, old building where there were more than enough children for a whole town of houses. Rebecca continually had awkward encounters with other orphans, probably because she rarely said anything.

In two years, she had become friendly with only two children her age—girls who shared her shyness when around others. But both moved away, while the sisters stayed and stayed, stuck in their room in the massive building.

As usual, Abby played on the floor with her doll while Rebecca sat on an old wooden stool, looking at the remaining bits of elaborate wallpaper that had not fully peeled and fallen. While again daydreaming about a better life, she was interrupted by one of the staff yelling in the hallway, "Get back to your room!" Most likely, a boy or girl had lingered too long on their way to or from the privy, the rough outdoor toilet room.

Rebecca was so grateful for Abby's sunshine personality that brought light into their days. Abby was always getting words mixed up, like calling caterpillars "pillarcasers." And then there were the ants. Abby had been fascinated with them since she was tiny. She'd sit for a long time intently watching them as they went about their business.

Which had led to one of the few moments of belly-hurting laughter since they'd arrived at the orphanage. The two sisters had been outside. Abby had played while Rebecca soaked in the warm sunshine.

After they got back in their room, Rebecca noticed that Abby kept squirming and scratching her stomach and legs. Rebecca soon discovered that her little sister had decided to bring her beloved ants inside with her by putting them in the secret pocket Rebecca had sewn inside her dress. They'd gradually crawled out, and Abby literally had ants in her pants. Rebecca had laughed the whole time they collected the tiny insects to put them back outside.

A sudden growl startled both girls. Rebecca's stomach had expressed her dissatisfaction from the previous night's stale bread and over-salted mashed potatoes. Horrible food was another thing that made Rebecca unhappy.

The terrible fruit for breakfast didn't count as a meal, especially since there wasn't enough for every child. Tolerable fruit at the orphanage was either soft, dark-spotted pears or wrinkly grapes, but at least that was better than the ever-present bowls of floppy, sour rhubarb sticks—or "wubawb sticks" as Abby called them.

Lunch and dinner were never any better, even less so because their mother had been an amazing cook, making tasty meals and delightful desserts. Sometimes as Rebecca chewed the tough mystery meat on the rare occasions they had it, she pretended she was still at home, eating chicken that was so tender it fell off the bone, flavorful gravy with no lumps, bread hot from the woodstove, and her mother's apple dumplings with fresh cream sauce. And the best part? All of it had been seasoned with love.

The tasteless food at the orphanage wasn't the only problem. The other children's mean comments often hurt Rebecca's feelings, but she couldn't fully blame them, because they were also stuck at the orphanage.

Mornings were filled with chores for all the orphans. Some had to wash dishes. Others did laundry out by the creek. The older girls had to put the food out for each meal, sweep up the crumbs left behind by all the children, and then get everything ready for the next meal.

Rebecca was so happy that her task was to help with the cows in the barn, because she could take Abby with her until she'd be old enough to do chores herself. She loved seeing how much Abby enjoyed the cats who kept the mice away in the barn. She played with them, laughing at how they purred when she petted them. That kept Abby busy while Rebecca put out fresh straw for the cows each day, fed them, and checked their hooves. Thankfully, one of the older boys did the milking, so Rebecca didn't have to get up even earlier for breakfast.

There was one other reason why Rebecca liked working with the cows. Those moments reminded her of sweet times when Father had let her go to the barn with him. One day he'd told her, "Rebecca, just as I take care of our cows, God takes care of all of us each day. He does that because He loves us, and He will *always* take care of you. Don't ever forget that."

Oh, how Rebecca wished Father could have told her more about God. Just like when she was hungry for food, there was something inside her that longed to know God better. She felt a bit of excitement well up. *Maybe I could make this my quest. I know the knights go out on quests for the king, journeys where they're on a mission to find something. I can't go anywhere on a journey, but perhaps I could make it my mission to learn more about God.* "Please, God, could you help me on my quest?"

When Rebecca and Abby had first arrived at the orphanage, they'd discovered a large building far different than the humble home they'd lived in. This once-fine manor house had been neglected after the owner had passed away. With no family members left to inherit it, the property had been signed over to the king, and he'd turned it into an orphanage for children in the kingdom who didn't have a home or parents to care for them.

Once the orphans finished their chores each day, they spent sunny afternoons out on the field next to the manor. Imaginations were put to good use there because that was the only option. Sticks from the forest became swords for the boys as they pretended to be knights. The young girls made believe that they were princesses living in a castle. And the younger children enjoyed races with their pretend stick ponies.

But about a year after Rebecca and Abby began living in the orphanage, something new was added for their play time. Now, along the edge of the woods that surrounded the field, there were some swings hanging from large tree branches.

The children were thankful, but they wished there were enough swings for all of them. They wouldn't even have the ones they had, though, if King Mesharet, leader of the kingdom, hadn't sent the building supplies, and some of his strong men from the castle to climb the trees and secure the swings in place.

During their first year at the orphanage, the sisters had soon learned there were no dolls, balls, or anything like that inside the entire building. But, somehow, the king had learned of the cheerless conditions at the home, and he'd sent handmade dolls, leather balls, books (a special treasure), fabric, needles, thread, and scissors to provide some joy and to keep the children busy.

Rebecca had been so happy to get the fabric and a needle and thread. That's how she had made the secret pockets inside her and Abby's dresses. Sometimes they were able to sneak a few bits of food into those pockets, so they'd have something to eat in their room when they were especially hungry. Rebecca also loved to find flowers in the field. She would often hide some in her secret pocket, and then she'd put them in their room to make it cheerier.

Today was one of the rainy days, and Abby sat playing on her bed. She adjusted the one hanging button that was the only eye on her only doll. Stuffing fell out from the hole left by a missing arm. Rebecca planned to mend the doll when she could borrow the needle and thread again.

At least Abby has a special doll, thought Rebecca. Their mother had made it, and the doll had once been beautiful, wearing pretty dresses that Mother had sewed for her. Abby liked to imagine the red-haired toy was a cyclops that would wreak havoc on the kings and queens painted onto the wallpaper in their room. Sometimes Rebecca pretended to be the princess who prevented the beast from terrorizing the kingdom.

Rebecca had learned to live with their tiny room covered with faded, torn remnants of sapphire-blue wallpaper. Each partial piece showed bits of a beautiful kingdom where smiling royals enjoyed their luxurious lives. It was nothing like the orphan life of the Faith sisters.

Memories of the past made the present even harder for Rebecca. Abby couldn't remember anything from home, but Rebecca remembered the comfortable bed with covers that smelled like sunshine and fresh air from where Mother had hung them on the clothesline.

At the orphanage, an ancient yellow rug stopped at a bed the sisters shared. The mattress was stained and lumpy, and almost flat from where the straw that was used to fill it had fallen out. The covers were rough and had holes in them, and everything smelled musty.

Lying mostly on hard wood and uncomfortable lumps brought sore bones that caused plenty of rolling over each night. The brown, scratched chest in their room had lost two of its four legs, resulting in an annoying tilt. Besides being able to sit on the floor and beds, the only other spot was a wooden stool that was taller than the tiny table it sat in front of, something Rebecca used as a much-too-small desk.

She tried to be strong and appear happy for Abby. She often described their days back at home for her sister, sharing about all the little things Mother had done to make life so special for them. She told Abby stories that Mother and Father had made up for them, wonderful tales of castles, princesses, and far-away places.

She loved hearing Abby laugh each time Rebecca shared about the day a tiny mouse had run through the house and their mother had screamed and jumped on the table. Father had taken the mouse outside, but he'd laughed until he had tears coming down his face.

Some days, Rebecca just wanted to cry at how different things were, but at the orphanage, there was nobody who cared, nobody who would comfort her.

Suddenly out in the hall someone yelled, "LUNCH TIME!"

The girls jolted upright at the sudden, loud shout. Now the race was on to get to the lunch line downstairs. Children launched out of over seventy rooms on the four floors. Nobody rushed because the food was good, but because all of them knew that the last children to arrive would get little to eat.

Rebecca and Abby gathered their food from the serving bowls. Meat was rare at the orphanage, but beans, cooked cabbage, and brown bread seemed to show up at lunch almost every day.

Suddenly, directly in front of Rebecca at the rectangular table, someone plopped onto the bench. Rebecca immediately gazed down, focusing on her food, but she knew she had never seen this girl before. As Rebecca swallowed hard on a first bite of lunch, the stranger cleared her throat, "Who are you? I'm Marie," the new girl said.

Rebecca dropped her spoon.

2

Some Hope

Marie waited as Rebecca picked up her spoon and used her sleeve to wipe away the splattered sauce from the table. But then when Rebecca still would not look up, the stranger asked again, "Well? What's your name?"

"Uhmmm … I'm Rebecca. And, ah, this is Ab—ah, my sister, Abby. Why?"

Rebecca thought Marie must be about her own age, but that was where the similarity ended. The stranger had an interesting, wild look, with lots and lots of red hair, freckles, and a bright, white grin.

Rebecca thought, *She looks friendly and her face sort of glows, but that wild look is going to make a lot of people stare at her. I would hate all that attention.*

"I was just wondering," Marie said, "because I was moved here a few days ago and I don't know anyone."

Rebecca half smiled and said, "Oh."

After a short, awkward silence, Marie added, "So, what do you like to do around here?"

"Uhmmm …" replied Rebecca, "I mostly read or sew, and I usually find things to do outside while my sister plays."

Marie said, "Oh, I love being outside. What have you found to do?"

Getting a tiny bit more comfortable with their unexpected lunch mate, Rebecca replied, "I watch Abby. Sometimes we go to the field and look to see if a swing is available, or we walk out to the stone fence at the edge of the forest, otherwise, not much."

Marie sat up straight and almost shouted with excitement, "Maybe we can spend time together after lunch. That is, if we're allowed out today. I've already done my chores this morning, so that's not a problem, but I'm still learning what we can and can't do."

Then Marie slouched back on the bench and added, "So far, the other children only look at me a lot and don't talk to me much. And the adults are always too busy."

Rebecca thought, *That explains why she's willing to talk to me.*

Rebecca added, "I guess we can do that."

The rest of lunch, the three girls mostly sat in silence, occasionally interrupted by Marie blurting something out, and Rebecca nodding in agreement. A few times Rebecca added, "Oh, hmm," or "uh-huh." Once she attempted a full sentence, but she was too nervous and kept saying words that made no sense, "Well, that's more … or, yes … ah, much … maybe … um …"

Rebecca's face took on an awkward grin because she was trying to appear relaxed. At first Marie smiled, but then cocked her head and seemed to struggle for words. Both girls gave up, looked down, and ate some more lunch.

When the sisters were finished eating, without looking up at Marie, Rebecca leaned toward her and pointed to the end of the room, "We're … um … we're supposed to … um … take our dishes—"

She trailed off as she and Abby rose to take their place in the long line of children who were dropping off spoons, bowls, and plates on a huge table. After each meal, the children added to the pile, steadily reshaping an enormous sculpture of food-covered metal and wood. Rebecca was always thankful that she wasn't one of the children who had to wash the dishes.

Marie stuffed her remaining lunch into her mouth, some of which flew back out when she attempted to delay the sisters. "Wae! I'll oo yoo."

Rebecca laughed out loud as Abby looked at her sister and asked, "What did she say?"

Marie gulped down her mouthful and restated what she had attempted to say, "Wait! I'll go too."

Marie jumped up and the three girls joined the line. As usual, Rebecca picked up her sister so Abby could place her dishes at the very top. Food stained her dress but Rebecca didn't worry about that because they were on their way outside. Abby's clothes would soon be much dirtier.

The three girls turned toward the door. Rebecca thought, *Why can't I think of anything to say? I would like to talk to this girl. She seems nice.* But it had been so long since anyone had been nice to

Rebecca that it was no wonder she couldn't remember how to have a normal conversation.

Marie and Abby grinned as the girls opened the door to go outside, but Rebecca was still too busy analyzing herself to say anything.

Rebecca tried to focus on something else. *I hope Abby doesn't want to play on the swings today. I can't watch her as closely with Marie talking to me.*

Unlike Abby, Rebecca dreaded their playtime. Some of the mean orphans shoved children to the ground if they wanted their swings. Rebecca still had deep purple and blue bruises from the last time she and Abby had been outside.

Rebecca constantly followed Abby to save her from harm, acting as a safety net for her sister's frequent falls. Abby got so used to the help that she sometimes jumped off the swing into her sister's arms on purpose. Rebecca had laughed the first few times.

Marie's gaze rapidly shot back and forth, scanning the area for what to do first. Her eyes settled on an empty swing. Rebecca touched her arm as Marie headed that way. "Not that one. It's broken." The story went that two big boys had stood together on the seat of the swing. They'd started swinging, but their combined weight had cracked the branch that held the swing, as well as breaking the wooden seat. They fell from high in the air, and orphans who saw it happen said both of them were seriously injured. One hadn't been seen since, and nobody had ever said if he was still alive or in a hospital.

Marie said, "Let's go sit and wait. Maybe a swing will become empty."

Walking toward the laughing swingers, the girls found a small patch of grass to sit on. Rebecca finally came up with something wonderfully interesting to tell Marie, an idea Rebecca had for an adventure, but one she would never be brave enough to do.

"Ever since the men put up the swings," began Rebecca, "I have wanted to swing with Abby. She's old enough now to kick her legs and get moving, which means we could each have our own swing. But it's hard to find even one open—let alone two—so I think it would be fun to wake up in the middle of the night, sneak downstairs, and swing all night. Then we could sleep during the afternoon, since there's not much to do anyway once we finish our chores."

Bursting with excitement, Marie jumped up, "Yes! Yes! Yes! Let's do it. How about tonight?"

Rebecca was shocked at Marie's explosive response. But before Rebecca could calm her down and stop Marie from announcing it to everyone around, a swing became available. Abby quickly put her arms around it. Rebecca followed behind, and then lifted Abby into the seat, and began pushing her, listening as her little sister squealed with excitement as the swing flew through the air.

The older sister thought, *I need to be careful about mentioning wild adventures to Marie. She's odd enough that she will want to do them.*

While Rebecca pushed and Abby laughed, Marie continued sitting nearby, a thoughtful smile on her face as if she was taking Rebecca's secret adventure idea and planning for something even wilder.

Rebecca worried, *Is this new girl too rowdy for Abby and me? And even if she's not, we're probably too quiet for her. She'll get tired of spending time with us.*

Still pushing Abby, Rebecca thought about how different Marie was from the rest of the children at the orphanage—and especially different from quiet, shy Rebecca. Marie was confident and talkative, and maybe she really was as wild as she seemed.

While Marie seemed nice and fun, Rebecca wasn't sure she could handle being around her too often. She suspected that Marie was going to be exhausting. She was just so unusual, bouncing around and asking a lot of questions.

Marie interrupted Rebecca's thoughts, "Can I push your sister?"

"Just please be careful."

Soon Abby and Marie were laughing, which also lifted Rebecca's spirits, reminding her again of how happy life had been with their parents. But that thought brought up a dreadful reality that had burdened Rebecca with guilt. Should she ever confess the dark, terrible secret about the death of their parents to Abby?

And if she did, when should she tell Abby? The most worrying question was whether her sister would hate her for what she did. It was a heavy secret for a young girl to keep to herself, but Abby was the only person she could confide in. Rebecca was afraid Abby would never speak to her again. Life was already hard enough without that happening.

Marie broke into her thoughts, "Do you want to go to the river? I found a beautiful place yesterday, with shallow water, and there are even steppingstones. I can show you."

Welcoming the distraction, Rebecca said, "Abby and I know that place. We've been there many times."

Seeing Marie's excitement fade, Rebecca quickly added, "It's a great place, though. Good idea, Marie. Let's go."

As they walked through a small patch of forest, neither Rebecca nor Abby said much, mostly because Marie talked the whole time. At one point Marie even counted the trees out loud.

As they walked through the quietness of the forest—well, other than Marie's endless stream of words—they reached the narrow brook. Marie sat on a rock near a small pool of water and said, "Hey, there are even more minnows today than yesterday."

Sitting next to Marie, Abby peered into the pool and matched Marie's wide-eyed enthusiasm, "Becky, she's right! There are so many. Can we take one back to the room this time?"

Rebecca gave her usual response. "We'll see, Abby. Maybe if you catch one."

"Yes!" said Abby, as she plunged a hand into the water and quickly closed it around a school of tiny fish. As always, the minnows easily darted away. Abby's lack of speed while reaching for the fish was why Rebecca said she could maybe keep it if she caught one.

Rebecca dreaded the day her sister would ask for help, but so far Abby hadn't, maybe because it looked easy. Rebecca worried that, one day, Abby would open that little fist and she would either find a squished fish, or a live one they would have to take back to their room—where it would die. And there was no telling what the orphanage workers would have to say if they found a fish in the girls' bedroom. Rebecca shivered just thinking about how angry they'd be. It wasn't pretty when they were upset.

Abby tried again, this time putting both hands in the water. Once more she closed her grip too tight and pulled her fists back out. In front of an eager Marie, Abby turned her hands over and opened her palms. Both girls were disappointed.

"Nothing," Abby said. "Why can't I get one?"

"Maybe you are getting them," said Marie, "but they are just invisible in the air."

While Abby reexamined her hands for invisible fish, Marie glanced at Rebecca, and the older girls laughed. Then Abby realized they were teasing her and joined in.

Marie turned to Rebecca, "How did you two end up here?"

A twinge of anxiety shot through Rebecca, "Our parents died in a fire."

Marie was silent long enough for Rebecca to change the subject, "What about your family?"

"I don't know what happened to my mother and father," said Marie. "Ever since I was a baby, I've always lived with strange adults and children. I mean, strangers to me—not family—though, I guess I'm probably strange to them. But I've always wondered what it would be like to have a real family that loved me."

Marie reworded her answer, "I've never known—or even heard stories about anyone in my family."

"I'm so sorry," said Rebecca. "It must be hard never having known your mother or father."

"Not really," said Marie, "I don't miss my parents because I never knew them."

There was a long silence while Rebecca thought about that answer. Even though she missed Mother and Father so much that she often cried herself to sleep, it would have been even sadder to have never known them.

Rebecca said, "Marie, I just remembered something my mother once told me. She said that we are all welcome to be part of the family of God, that He is our Father and he will always love us. I wish I could tell you how to join His family, but that's all I know."

Even Marie sat there quietly for a bit as they all thought about that. A few minutes later, Rebecca asked, "Were those other places you were at 'slum dumps' like this one?"

Marie laughed at Rebecca's name for the orphanage, which made the sisters laugh too. And then Rebecca explained, "One day while I was watching Abby play on the floor in our room, she suddenly stopped, looked around, and began sort of singing, 'Slum dump, slum dump … slum dump, slum dump … slum dump, slum dump.' Even after she went back to playing, she continued to say the words for a while. I didn't know if she was talking about the orphanage, but I thought it was perfect, so we've used it ever since."

The girls laughed some more, until Abby asked Marie, "Do you have other friends?"

"Yes," Marie said, as her smile became sad, "but I don't know where they are. I make friends at the homes where I'm placed, but then the adults send me away, and my friends aren't allowed to come with me. My friends were the closest thing I had to family—or at least what I think a family would be like—and I really miss them."

This was the first real sadness Rebecca had seen from Marie. Rebecca touched the pool of water to start more ripples and said, "I wish *no one* would *ever* lose their friends or family."

Suddenly angry, Marie agreed, "Me too. If God can fix anything, why does He do that?"

Rebecca replied, "I don't know. Maybe we'll find out someday."

"Well, let's ask someone." said Marie.

"I don't know anyone here who would know about God," Rebecca replied.

They were silent again until Marie asked if the sisters wanted to explore some more. The girls were happy to, especially Abby who was quite frustrated at the disappearing minnows. They walked around awhile, but kept running into the tall stone fence, an impenetrable-looking barrier that surrounded the sides and back of the orphanage property. Beyond the fence were forest, hills, and mountains.

Eventually they returned to the field for the rest of the afternoon, and then ate dinner together. But, thankfully, this time, talkative Marie managed to keep all her food in her mouth.

Later that night, Rebecca lay awake on her uncomfortable mattress, thinking about their day. *I really like Marie, and being friends with her might make the slum dump more interesting and fun. But what if Abby and I grow to like her a lot and then she gets sent away? That's probably just what will happen.*

As the moon rose higher in the sky, and the minutes ticked by, Rebecca continued to think, *So maybe for Abby's sake, we shouldn't become friends with Marie. We've been fine keeping to ourselves, and we don't need more loss in our lives. Besides, Marie will easily find other friends, so we don't even need to feel guilty about it.*

Before finally drifting off to dreams of dragons, exciting quests, castles, princes, and princesses, a more serious concern kept Rebecca awake a bit longer, *What if the adults sent Marie away from those other orphanages because she's dangerous?*

(**3**)

A Royal Visitor

Because her mind whirled with thoughts at bedtime, Rebecca fell asleep not much before dawn and woke later than normal. That meant the sisters were tardy for breakfast.

Rebecca sprang up, "Abby, hurry. The good fruit will be gone, and we might not even get any rhubarb."

Still sleepy, the older sister changed into her dress, and pulled the door open. But as she saw all the children going back to their rooms from breakfast, Rebecca said, "There's no use going down now. Everything will be gone."

"But I'm hungwy!" Abby protested. So the sisters ran downstairs, where it only took a few minutes for Rebecca to discover she'd been right. Nothing was left in the huge, wooden serving bowls.

"Can we go outside and pick wubawb?" Abby asked. "We could eat it raw. My stomach hurts because I'm so hungwy."

Rebecca would have liked to, but she said, "No, Abby, you heard the announcement last night. We have to stay inside until after a special visitor leaves."

The girls trudged back to their room. Rebecca read for a while, and Abby played on the floor with her doll until a man in the hall called for everyone to line up. As was customary with special visitors, the children would be marched downstairs in an orderly manner.

The sisters opened their door to the usual chaos of a single adult trying to line up forty children—a task that was sometimes like herding cats. Rebecca tried to stay away from trouble, so when she saw a couple of cooperative orphans, she reached for Abby's hand, "Come on, let's go stand behind those children at the top of the stairs."

As usual, the rebellion was allowed to go on way too long, but ended when the man near the steps raised his voice and said, "LINE UP FOR PRINCESS MIRRA!" That got everyone's attention. The orphans loved the princess. She was so beautiful—and she was always nice to them.

Once the man had some semblance of order, he said, "We are going to walk slowly down to the dining hall. When there, you will find a seat quickly. While Princess Mirra is speaking, you *will* be silent! Do as you're told. No complaining. And smile."

Rebecca turned to Abby and whispered, "I've never seen him smile."

Too excited to catch her sister's teasing, Abby shouted, "THE PWINCESS! THE PWINCESS!"

Abby often talked about wanting to be a princess, probably because Rebecca had always enjoyed reading royal stories about the adventures of knights, queens, princes, princesses, castles, quests, scary forests, and all other aspects of kingdom lands. She even made up some of her own tales to tell Abby.

The truth was that Rebecca also held an unspoken wish that she too could one day become a real princess. It was a longing for both girls, fueled by the scraps of wallpaper remaining on the walls of their tiny room. Rebecca longed for a happy and luxurious royal life as shown in the broken scenes on the walls.

Day after day, Rebecca looked at the wallpaper, often focusing on the handsome princes, most with dark hair. One after another, she would imagine each prince unexpectedly showing up on his mighty horse, arriving at their slum dump and running upstairs to knock on her door, determined to win Rebecca's heart and transform her dreary life.

Upon seeing him, it would be love at first sight for Rebecca, and the honorable boy would pledge his total devotion to her. He would escort both sisters downstairs and outside, sweeping them up onto his horse, and carrying them off to his family's huge and magnificent castle. There, he and Rebecca would someday be married. Later, Abby would marry his little brother, and they would all live amazing, joyful lives.

But Rebecca was well aware that her daydreams weren't reasonable, so her thoughts would always end with the reality of her life. *I'm too old to believe that,* she would tell herself. *And our family has had no kings, queens, or other royal blood, so why would a prince ever show up for me?*

Not wanting to disappoint Abby, Rebecca kept that realization about family bloodlines to herself. But regardless of their own limitations toward reaching royal status, they both liked the kindhearted princess who was visiting that day.

The sisters had seen Princess Mirra on her last two visits over the past couple years, though Abby was too young to remember much about her. Rebecca decided the princess must be at least eight or ten years older than her, but it was hard to tell for sure with all her fancy clothes and jewelry, such as the beautiful, sparkly crown sitting on Mirra's long brown hair.

Abby asked, "Becky, is the pwincess going to talk to all of us?"

"Yes, I'm sure she will," said Rebecca. "At least once per year, the kingdom's royal guards bring her to check on our living conditions to see if we are being treated well by the sour-natured adults here.

Abby scrunched her eyes in intense concentration, "Maybe when she sees how bad it is, she'll take us to her castle."

"No, Abby," Rebecca laughed. "We're certainly not going to the castle. That's where the king and queen live, not us."

The man at the head of the line said, "Okay, let's go—but *slowly*—and stay in order."

Near the front of the line, Rebecca and Abby arrived at the dining hall with the second-floor orphans. The first-floor children, who were some of the youngest at the orphanage, had already taken their seats.

After Rebecca, Abby, and the children from their floor sat, the older orphans from the top two floors took the rest of the tables, but many ended up standing because there were not enough spots left.

Once the residents from every floor had arrived, the stern-looking headmistress shouted, "QUIET! QUIET DOWN! QUIET!" The room became silent and she continued, "In a moment or two, Her Royal Highness Princess Mirra will arrive to make a few remarks and will then allow a couple of questions. Once she has finished speaking and left the room—AND NOT UNTIL THEN—you will go back to your rooms and remain there until she finishes her tour. Applaud when appropriate, but until then, STAY QUIET."

Turning to her sister, Abby said, "I don't like the headmistress lady."

Rebecca nodded in agreement, as she thought back to the princess's last visit, when Rebecca had overheard Mirra in the hallway, scolding the adults for the pitiful conditions at the dump, especially their filthy dining hall. Some improvements happened after her visit, but they didn't last long.

Rebecca looked around, *It actually looks clean,* she thought. *I bet the adults stayed up all night mopping and scrubbing the greasy floors and sticky tables. Why didn't they make us children do it this time? Perhaps they thought we'd fall asleep in front of the princess.*

As she finished that thought, Princess Mirra entered and the children erupted in cheers. Like previous visits, Rebecca thought how overwhelmingly elegant and beautiful the princess was, with her wide smile, silky brown hair, and bright green eyes.

Also wonderful was her gracious, kind manner with the children. Princess Mirra did not waste it on the sour-faced adults. Her diamond-filled crown and other jewelry sparkled around her glowing face. She seemed to float through the room in her floor-length, blue and yellow dress.

Walking slowly, she spent quite a while making eye contact with the youngest children, many of whom would probably never forget it. Then she turned without acknowledging the headmistress next to her and waited for the buzz of excitement to die down.

When the room was calm, she glided to the front, turned, and addressed the room, "For those who are new here, I am Princess Mirra. King Mesharet and Queen Narissa have me visit every orphanage in the land to learn whether the adults are taking good care of the kingdom's beloved children. Though your surroundings may seem bleak, we make sure you have a home, clothes, and food. In return, His Majesty only asks that you try to be kind and helpful to others, which is what makes God happy.

"While you are here, we hope you find new friends and learn skills that will help when you're grown, married, and have a house and children of your own. Life is full of problems, such as dealing with unhappy people—"

She glanced quickly at the headmistress.

"But we must all remain grateful to God—who loves us dearly—for creating us and making us each one of a kind. By loving God and others, you will eventually have a blessed life. Maybe not today, but someday it will happen if you stay faithful."

Those comments made Rebecca wonder, *Can my life really improve? Is happiness possible again without my mother and father?*

The princess finished, thanked the children for listening, and smiled when they again broke out in applause.

But her dazzling smile dimmed upon motioning for the headmistress to walk forward. The woman made it to the front and the room became quiet. With slight irritation in her voice, Princess Mirra briefly addressed her, "Thank you for your service. Please leave now. Do not return."

The woman sputtered, "Yes, we … uhm, you—"

"Thank you," added the princess. "That will be all."

Once the headmistress left, the young royal turned toward the remaining adults standing at the back wall. "Though it appears clean now, my aides report that this place's normal condition is filthy, and that is only the start of the issues here. Therefore, the castle craftsmen and I will assess the level of disrepair and provide the gold needed to purchase materials for a list of renovations.

"You will acquire those items locally, including what is needed for a recreation area for the children. We will return in three days to see that you have obtained everything, and you will be given one month to make the changes. Should you fail, the kingdom will find other caretakers, and *all* of you will be out."

Princess Mirra's smile returned when she faced the boys and girls, "I am sorry, children, but because this situation requires an extra-thorough inspection, and I have other, urgent matters in nearby towns, I cannot take your questions at this time."

She looked back at the adults, "Please show me around."

The orphans applauded one more time, and Rebecca smiled at seeing her little sister clapping wildly and jumping up and down. With awe coloring her voice, Abby said, "Oh, Becky! The pwincess is beautiful!"

4

An Odd Illness

The children were sent back to their rooms to wait during the princess's inspection. Rebecca became increasingly concerned that Abby was talking less and had been coughing a bit, so she felt Abby's forehead. It was hot. When the children were finally allowed out of their rooms, the sisters remained, allowing Rebecca to keep an eye on Abby's symptoms.

Then came a knock at the door. Because adults mostly only yelled from the hall, Rebecca was worried as she slowly opened the door. But it was only Marie, and she too looked concerned.

Marie asked, "Rebecca, are you and Abby okay? I didn't see you earlier, and then you weren't outside, so I thought I'd better come check."

"Yes, we're fine," Rebecca replied, "How did you find our room?"

"I asked an adult," Marie explained. "Are you sure nothing is wrong? Why aren't you outside?"

"Well, actually, Abby isn't feeling well," answered Rebecca. "I'm hoping it won't get worse."

"Oh, that's terrible," said Marie. "Let me take a look at her."

Uninvited, Marie walked right past Rebecca, went to the bed, felt Abby's forehead, and turned back to Rebecca with a disturbed look on her face, "Some children at my table this morning were talking about a little boy and really young girl who are terribly sick, so maybe Abby caught something while we were eating, or when we were outside with the other children."

Horrified, Rebecca exclaimed, "We have to tell the adults."

"We can go see the nurse," said Marie.

Rebecca was already on her way to get Abby and carry her out the door. The three went downstairs and all the way to the other end of the first floor, where the nurse's door was open. With most everyone outside, there were no children around, and no patients waiting.

It was a tiny room with a stool, a chest, and a small bed where Rebecca put Abby. The atmosphere here was even more unwelcoming than the rest of the orphanage. Not knowing if they should also sit on the bed, the older girls stood and waited for what felt like an hour.

When the nurse finally walked in, she looked at them in annoyance and said, "Yes? What do you want?"

Rebecca thought her horrible manners were probably because of a lack of sleep from being up cleaning all night. But her eyes were mean, and her whole face looked like she'd swallowed something sour, so maybe she was like that all the time.

Rebecca pointed at Abby, "It's my sister. She's sick."

The nurse extended a hand and felt Abby's forehead, "Hmmm. No, she feels fine. Come back when she's really sick."

"But—"

Crossing her arms, the woman interrupted, "I am too busy to treat every bump, bruise, sniffle, headache, scratchy throat, and imaginary illness. Now go, and only come back if she gets much, much worse."

Rebecca exchanged shocked glances with Marie and let out a defeated sigh. The building had too many orphans for one over-worked nurse. Rebecca knew her sister's sickness might be serious, but she was not brave enough to confront the mean woman. Instead, she picked Abby up and Marie followed them out of the woman's office.

Partway down the hall, Marie stopped at a door, "Here's my room, Rebecca. I know Abby needs rest, so I'll see you two later, but please let me know if she gets worse."

"I will," Rebecca agreed. The sisters struggled on down the hallway.

In their room, Rebecca found it hard to concentrate with Abby's cough getting deeper and more frequent. Her sister was so still and pale, and it scared her. Abby was never still. The older sister waited an excruciating hour, left her sister to rest, and headed back to the nurse's office to report Abby's worsening condition.

Again, the room was empty. The nurse walked in a little later, and immediately wagged her finger at Rebecca, "You quit bothering me. Your sister can't be much worse. Stop wasting my time. Get out of here and go outside."

What a ridiculous suggestion, thought Rebecca. *Who would watch Abby?*

Exhausted with worry, but also gripped with fear of this horrible woman, Rebecca trudged back to her and Abby's room. Moments like this made their situation at the orphanage even harder. *Mother would have known what to do,* she thought. *I'm trying hard to take good care of Abby, but I'm still just a child myself.*

Abby's condition continued going downhill as the day went by. Rebecca felt like food might help, so at dinner time she ran to the dining hall and brought back stew. But even that was hard for Abby with her sore throat. Despite Rebecca's encouragement, Abby ate just one or two little bites. Rebecca sat beside her on the bed, wondering what to do.

After the sun set, she decided the nurse would have to help when she saw how pitiful Abby had become. Rebecca picked up her pale, coughing sister and carried her all the way to the nurse's door.

With all the worry, Rebecca forgot her promise to tell Marie if Abby got worse, so the sisters went right by Marie's room and came to the closed door of the nurse's office.

Rebecca wondered, *Is she with a patient? Or maybe she's gone back to her room to sleep.*

Much alarmed and frantic about her little sister's declining condition, Rebecca had to find out, so she turned the knob, opened the door, and found the nurse slumped over on the bed. Rebecca's first, terrifying thought was that the spreading disease had already killed the woman. But by the time Rebecca realized she was only sleeping, Abby's sniffling and coughing caused the nurse to jerk awake and almost fall off the bed. She snarled at the girls, "I told you to quit bothering me. Are you deaf?"

But Rebecca wouldn't take no for an answer. "Please, ma'am, my sister is really sick and I'm so concerned about her." After a few moments of looking back and forth at the faces of both girls, the frowning woman reached out, felt Abby's forehead and said, "It's a fever."

Horribly worried, and no longer concerned about the consequences, Rebecca boldly said, "We have to get her a doctor."

The woman paused to ponder that idea, and then replied, "It's too late tonight for someone to come all this way in the dark, but I'll give your sister something to help her sleep. We'll fetch a doctor in the morning."

Abby's face scrunched while struggling to swallow the nurse's nasty spoonful of medicine. Rebecca didn't know what else she could do, so she picked up her sister, said nothing more to the nurse, and walked down the dark hall toward Marie's room. She stopped, but did not knock, remembering how late it was. She decided Marie might be asleep, so they continued upstairs.

Once more carrying Abby, worries flooded Rebecca's mind, *Should I have awakened Marie? She was really concerned about Abby. What's wrong with my sister? I've already lost everybody else I love.*

Her sister felt so hot, and she barely responded when Rebecca spoke to her. Tears streamed down Rebecca's face. Her thoughts ran wild again. *Will that grouchy nurse keep her promise to get the doctor? What if the doctor can't help? I love my sister. What if she doesn't make it? What would I do without her? I'd be all alone in the world.*

Reaching the room, Rebecca put Abby to bed. She coughed a little longer before finally falling asleep. Rebecca lay awake pondering her questions, until a comforting thought finally helped her fall asleep, *Other children are sick too, so the nurse* has *to get a doctor.*

5

The Dreadful Forest

Rebecca woke while it was still dark and climbed from their bed. She shivered. Their room was always chilly, but especially in the mornings. She worried as she saw Abby had kicked the thin blanket off in her sleep.

Rebecca pulled the blanket around her little sister, leaned in for a closer look, and listened to her breathing. There was a raspy sound that hadn't been there the night before. Her sleep was restless, and Abby had moaned throughout the night.

While Abby was still sleeping, Rebecca dressed quickly and headed downstairs. She was on a mission to be first in line for fruit that might help her sick sister. After standing in line a while, she was finally able to snatch an apple, banana, and even a rarely-seen nectarine.

Reaching the second floor, she could hear Abby coughing, and when she opened the door to their room, the sunlight coming through the window revealed her sister's sickly, colorless face. She asked Abby how she was feeling, but the little girl was too sleepy and weak to talk. Hoping food would help, Rebecca peeled the banana and put it and the nectarine in front of Abby, keeping only the apple for herself.

She wanted to rush Abby down to the nurse, but was concerned that the woman might get angry and not send for the doctor if she had not called for one already. Rebecca decided to give the doctor a little more time to reach them.

But Abby only made it through half of the banana before breaking into the longest coughing fit Rebecca had heard yet. Rebecca got up, ran out the door to the stairs, skipped every other one jumping down the steps to the first floor, dashed through the long hallway, and reached the nurse's office in record time—only to wait in the hall while two other children were being examined.

When it was finally her turn, Rebecca stepped inside. Without even saying good morning, she asked, "Do you know when the doctor will get here?"

"You again?" said the immediately annoyed nurse. "The doctor isn't coming. I only told you that last night so we could all get some rest. Your sister will be fine. Stop bothering me. Go!"

Stunned and horrified, and without even thinking about it, Rebecca shouted, "MY SISTER IS SICK! WHY DON'T YOU CARE?"

Coldly, the nurse replied, "Just keep her in bed. She'll sleep it off."

"PLEASE!" Rebecca pleaded.

But the woman only shook her head and pointed her bony finger out the door, "Go back to your room—and don't come back."

Furious, Rebecca stormed out and down the hall, attracting stares from other children as she made her way to Marie's door. Rebecca knocked. When there was no answer, she stomped the rest of the way to her and Abby's room.

There, she explained the desperate situation to her sister, "I'm sorry Abby, but the mean, horrible nurse still refuses to get a doctor."

Abby coughed a few times and whispered, "Why, Becky?"

"I don't know," answered Rebecca. "I guess she just doesn't care."

At that, Abby perked up the slightest little bit and suggested something surprisingly wiser than her age, "Well then, why don't we just go to the doctor?"

Rebecca didn't take the idea seriously at first, but then she couldn't stop thinking about it, and before long, her extreme concern for Abby turned it into a real option. She thought, *The nurse won't do anything, and the other adults will just tell us to go see the nurse.*

After agonizing over the idea for five or ten minutes—while Abby continued coughing—Rebecca decided it could be the only way to get help. Then over the next half hour, she came up with a plan. But immediately, doubts crept in.

I can't do this! she said to herself. *Of all the orphans who might run away, no one would ever think of Abby and me doing something like that.* Tears sprang to Rebecca's eyes as she whispered quietly, "Oh, Mother! I've never needed you more. I don't know how to do this. I don't know how to keep Abby alive and well."

Then she softly said, "God, our father once told me that on bad days we could bring our burdens to you. Will you please take care of my sister? She's so little and so sick."

Rebecca sat down and started thinking about what she needed to do to get help for her sister. The plan wasn't complicated, but bringing along a very sick four-year-old could make it impossible. Panic clawed at her throat as all the things that could go wrong flashed through her mind. But Abby *had* to have help.

She told Abby, "Once we're let out of the building at lunch, we'll head through the forest to the fence at the edge of the property. I can use a pair of scissors to poke through the stuff that surrounds the stones. I'm not sure if the scissors will work, but we have to try. From there we'll go through the forest, so we won't be seen on the road. Town is only a few hills and couple of miles, and then we'll ask people where the hospital is. Surely someone will help us."

Removing the dried mud around the stones was a huge concern, but Rebecca was more worried about the stories of how orphanages punished runaways. She heard runaway orphans were sent to detention facilities which were much more horrible than the slum dump. Rebecca's plan was to return before the sisters were missed.

She thought, *The adults won't notice we're gone because they usually ignore us anyway. But am I making a big mistake? Abby's had a lot of sleep, even though most of it was restless. But being so sick, can she walk that far to town? I can't carry her most of the way through the woods. Should we really do this? It seems foolish.*

But she quickly came back to the realization that they had no other choice. She loved Abby dearly and would get her help, just as their mother and father would have expected her to.

A little later that day, their journey began. Just before their normal lunchtime, the girls left their room and headed downstairs toward the dining hall. Rebecca thought about knocking on Marie's door, but decided she'd better not.

Marie may be too loud and unpredictable to keep our secret, Rebecca thought. *And I don't want to get her in trouble and moved again—this time to a detention home.*

Near the front of the line, Rebecca picked up plenty of food, which included soup for Abby since it would be the easiest for her to eat. They sat at the first table. Rebecca ate a few bites, and then she turned her attention to helping Abby eat between coughing fits.

Abby was still slowly sipping soup when Rebecca saw orphans already going outside. They had to hurry before too many children left the building, so Rebecca had Abby take one more spoonful of warm soup and shuffled her over to drop off their dishes.

Knowing the adults were busy with lunch, Rebecca left Abby at the door and ran to the office of the headmistress who had been fired. There she took some scissors and hid them in the folds of her dress. With her heart pounding out of her chest, she quickly made it back to Abby. They walked out the door and straight into the woods.

When they reached the stone fence, Rebecca closed the scissor blades and pushed through the hardened mud, or whatever it was, as hard as she could, but nothing happened. She gripped the scissors with both hands and applied pressure with all her might—but still nothing. She took a short break, and then went back at it, this time trying to surprise the mud by poking it suddenly. Still nothing.

Normal scissors seemed to be no match for the sturdy barrier blocking their way to get Abby help. Despair gripped Rebecca as she looked at her sister and thought about how she was letting Abby and their parents down. She went back at the hard mud again, this time using the scissor blades as a saw, pressing and pushing back and forth. But when she stopped and looked, there were only shallow scratches.

With tears of frustration and failure rolling down her cheeks, Rebecca sat next to Abby. She stared at the stone fence for a moment, and then hung her head. "God, if you're listening, we need help!" While she spent the next few minutes deciding what she would say on her next visit to the nurse, Abby walked down the fence line toward the stream with the minnows.

Suddenly Abby stopped and pointed, "Becky, look."

Way down the barrier, just before it disappeared into another patch of woods, Abby had spotted where a huge tree had fallen, toppling the stone fence to the ground. Jumping up, Rebecca dropped the scissors, ran to Abby, and picked her up in celebration. Abby got too excited and began another coughing fit, so Rebecca sat her down until she quieted, and then she led her sister along the fence, completely forgetting about the borrowed scissors.

Arriving at the toppled tree, they discovered that the huge branches were easy to walk through, so for the first time in two years, they stepped outside the property limits. Rebecca picked Abby up and hurried to get deeper into the trees, before they could be seen by other orphan explorers.

They soon plunged into thick forest, which turned out to be much scarier than Rebecca had anticipated when she picked that route to avoid being seen. Briars and thorns reached out to them as they pushed their way through, leaving scratches and spots of blood. Even though she tried to be careful, Rebecca had received several hard slaps on the face from tree branches she didn't see in time.

Rebecca hadn't worried about finding their way to town, because there was a tall tower there that the children could always see when they climbed trees or swung really high. They couldn't see the tower through the tree branches while walking through the forest, but Rebecca still thought she could lead them in the right direction to find it.

But she and sickly Abby were not the least prepared for the rough, hilly terrain and other perilous obstacles—like what lived in those dark, dense woods. Rebecca startled every time she heard a noise. *Was that a wild animal, or did something heavy fall in the woods?* Right away, Rebecca realized dresses were terrible for traveling through thick forest.

Making matters worse, recent rain had created swampy, muddy traps that kept the girls from taking the flatter, easier routes. The only way to avoid some of the mud was to struggle through thickets of thorny bushes and other snarled undergrowth. Rebecca carried Abby when she could, but mostly held her hand as they progressed slowly, and stopped whenever Abby's cough got really bad, or she had to rest.

Each step pushing through the prickly plants left more tears in their dresses, tears in their eyes, and red slashes on their arms and legs. Another problem was the plentiful bugs landing on them, tiny biters that seemed to multiply rapidly as they informed their friends that free meals were walking by. Rebecca thought the winged demons were also alerting the crawly insects on the ground that were jumping aboard and biting the sisters' legs.

Rebecca stayed in front, protecting Abby from the sticky cobwebs that were building up on Rebecca's front side and in her hair. The webs full of twigs and leaves soon doubled the size of Rebecca's head. The couple of times that Abby ended up in front, she wasn't tall enough to hit most of the webs, so the older sister got them anyway. And the little sister would push through tree branches, unknowingly letting them snap back, whipping her big sister.

After they'd gone quite a way into the forest, Rebecca decided this day might end up being the worst of her life—other than losing their parents—and certainly would be if the sisters died there. But Abby's bravery impressed her. The tough little girl marched on, suffering through severe sickness and the awful forest. All the while, Rebecca knew Abby was quickly losing strength.

As Rebecca began wondering if she should try carrying Abby the rest of the way, her little sister tripped, dropped Rebecca's hand, fell down a hill, and landed in some deep, swampy mud. Rebecca lunged forward and jumped down the hill to pull Abby out, but lost her balance and fell in herself. Swimming in muck, the stronger sister worked at keeping both of their faces out of the smelly sludge.

Suddenly Rebecca stopped struggling when she heard a loud crash close by, like the breaking of a large branch.

Abby had apparently heard it too. "Becky, what is it?" asked Abby, turning to her older sister with a look of alarm on her mud-covered face.

Neither girl could see over the hill to know what sort of creature it might be—but it sounded large. Rebecca concealed her panic, "Abby, just stay still and if you need to cough, please, please do it quietly. We're so covered with mud in this hole that it will probably pass right by and not see us."

But the crashing and snapping wood got closer and closer until Rebecca pulled herself and Abby deeper into the pool of muck so that only their faces stuck out. The forest monster's movements grew louder and louder until it had to be just over the little hill. Terrified and desperate, Rebecca feared they might need to sink all the way under, until it passed.

But would Abby be able to hold her breath? Rebecca wondered.

She decided they had to try and that each would go under and count to ten before coming back out. She whispered, "Abby, we need to—"

Snap! A large branch broke. *Crash!* Something fell. "AAARR-RGH!" screamed the monster.

The sisters looked at each other.

"It's a person." said Rebecca. "But who?" She pulled herself and Abby out of the mud, scrambled quietly up the little hill, and looked over the top. Sticking up from the broken branches of an old, fallen tree were two muddy legs.

Ready to take Abby and run if needed, Rebecca shouted, "Are you hurt?"

A voice came back, "Rebecca?"

Stunned, the older sister staggered forward and looked down into the tree. There lay Marie, with a gigantic mass of red tangles and the same sort of muddy, filthy, scratched, and bruised body as the sisters.

"Marie?" said Rebecca.

"It's you. I'm so glad it's you!" shouted Marie, struggling in the branches to pull herself upright.

Rebecca reached down for her hand, and after much work from both of them, Marie made it out onto solid ground.

"Thank you," said Marie, "And there's Abby. I am so relieved to find you two."

Abby said, "Marie, you look awful!"

"So do we, Abby," said Rebecca. "We're glad to see you, Marie. But how … why in the world are *you* here?"

Marie had a lot to say about that. Of course she did. "Well, first thing this morning I came to check on Abby, but you didn't answer the door so I thought maybe I had the wrong one. I started knocking on all the doors, and pretty soon an adult saw me, got mad, and said I had to stay in my room until lunch. Stuck there, I fell asleep until I heard children in the hall when lunch started.

"I ran down the hall to the lunch room, looked around, and saw you going out the door. I figured I should get some food while I could, and then find you outside. But when I came out, you weren't out on the field, so I went looking for you in the forest.

"After you weren't at the stream, I kept searching, and noticed some boys playing at a tree that had fallen over the fence. I went to ask if they had seen two girls. One of them told me he had seen a couple of girls cross the fence and go into the woods.

"So, I climbed over and saw two sets of footprints in the mud— one my size and the other smaller. I thought they were probably yours, so I followed them. It was *so* hard in this dreadful, sticky, scary forest. With Abby being so sick, I don't know how she's done it."

Marie paused, but the sisters said nothing, still shocked that she was standing there. Marie spoke again, "Where are you two going? How is Abby? Why didn't you let me know how Abby's been doing? Why did you leave without me?"

Not waiting for answers, she continued, "I kept following your footprints because I feared something terrible had happened, and I wanted to help. I would have gone along. I always want to help. And lots of orphans try to escape, so I have some experience with it."

Marie exhausted herself, so Rebecca finally had a chance to respond. "Marie, Abby is getting worse. Look at her. There's no color in her face. She's coughed until she can't catch her breath, and she's feverish. And the adults don't care. The mean nurse wouldn't help at all."

"Oh, no," said Marie. "We need to get her to a doctor."

"That's where we're going."

Marie walked over and picked up Abby. With the older girls taking turns carrying Abby, the muddy, bitten, bruised, scraped, and scratched orphans struggled toward a bit of distant light that looked like the end of the dreadful forest. They eventually reached the edge of the woods and sat down in the grass to rest. Right away Rebecca noticed that a stream was blocking their way to town.

She turned to point it out to the other two, but Marie had already jumped up and started running downhill. The sisters watched and soon stood as Marie gained speed down the hill. Their mouths dropped open when Marie didn't slow down near the bottom. She actually sped up as she approached the shore of the stream, and then jumped into the air, throwing herself at a large pool of water, and landing with a huge splash.

Even though both of them were beyond exhausted by this point, the muddy sisters couldn't help laughing before Rebecca picked up her sister and hobbled down the hill to join their friend. By the time

they reached where Marie was washing up, she looked like herself again. Rebecca and Abby waded in to clean themselves. Abby stayed in the shallower water and the older girls kept an eye on her until all three had washed off most of the dreadful mud and forest tokens from their journey.

Together they reached the other side and emerged soaking wet, but the sun was out during that hottest part of the day, and they still had a short walk to town. Abby walked until just outside of town, and then had another lengthy coughing fit that took every last bit of energy from her. The other two were also beaten up and exhausted, but they again took turns carrying her. Worry spurred them on to find the hospital.

6

The Hospital

With their wild hair and wet, stained and torn dresses, the girls attracted stares as they walked down one side of a wide, cobblestone street. Rebecca marveled at the activity of so many busy townspeople rushing everywhere, and children playing beside the streets. Well-dressed people walked briskly by.

Probably going somewhere important, Rebecca thought.

Between the houses were booths and carts where farmers sold eggs, chickens, and a variety of vegetables. One booth had freshly-baked loaves of bread for sale. A cart was loaded with handmade tools for purchase. But the girls didn't see a hospital anywhere.

"Excuse me. *Excuse* me! EXCUSE ME!" persisted Marie from behind two elderly men dressed in fine attire.

They turned and looked the girls up and down. Marie asked, "Can you please tell us where the hospital is?"

The men were silent for a few more moments, but then one volunteered the information quite precisely, "Go past two crossroads and turn left at the third. Turn right at the next crossroad. There you will see a hospital with a large wooden cross above the door. If we weren't on our way to take care of some business, we'd take you safely there. Your little one doesn't look well. Is she—"

Not meaning to be rude—just extremely tired and worried about Abby—the girls were already walking past the men. Their "Thank you, sirs!" drifted behind them. Upon making the second turn, they saw the hospital, a colossal building with many steps, six enormous columns, and a large door with a huge, fat cross above it. Rebecca thought how much grander it must have been at one time, before the old exterior had become somewhat dirty and faded. As her heart rejoiced about finally getting help for her little sister, Rebecca whispered, "I've never seen anything so beautiful."

Getting closer, she noticed a thick layer of greenish-brown moss on the shaded areas. Rebecca and Marie teamed up to open one of the two matching doors and found a cheery interior with light shining in from the windows, as well as some candles and fireplaces burning. Taking Abby by the hand, Rebecca walked toward a table where a kind-looking woman sat.

"Hello, ma'am," Rebecca said.

She replied, "Well, hello, children. What are the three of you doing here by yourselves? Where are your parents?"

Ignoring her question, Rebecca said, "It's my sister. She's sick and we're so worried about her. We don't know what she has, but it has gotten much, much worse over the last two days. She needs a doctor right away."

"I see," said the woman, "What is your sister's name?"

"Abby ... um, Abigail," said Rebecca.

Marie added, "And this is Rebecca, and I'm Marie."

"And where are your parents?" said the woman. "I assume you have their permission to be here?"

"We don't—" started Marie.

Rebecca cut her off, not trusting what she might reveal.

"We saw how sick she is and hurried to bring her in ourselves," said Rebecca. "We were so concerned we were afraid to wait."

Rebecca was happy to have avoided lying. The woman looked them over for a few moments, got a slight smile on her face, and addressed Abby, "Miss Abigail, right this way, please."

Abby stretched out her arms for Rebecca to pick her up. Instead, the woman took Abby's hand. They turned down the hall toward a wheeled chair. Abby's eyes lit up.

"Becky, look!" she said weakly, while climbing onto the chair.

Marie squeezed in front of Rebecca and reached for the handles to push Abby. Initially, the woman stepped forward like she meant to replace Marie, but then seemed to change her mind and let the girls enjoy the unusual chair. The woman led them down a long hallway and into a large room where she had Abby stretch out on a bed and directed the other two girls toward chairs.

Sinking into hers, Marie said, "These are the softest pillows I have ever sat on."

Rebecca agreed, and despite her concern for Abby, the next half hour became a blur of the two older girls fading in and out of sleep. Rebecca barely noticed when the nurses and doctors came in to look at Abby, but at one point when she was awake, a doctor asked Abby about her bruises. Rebecca was relieved when Abby just babbled something about bugs and trees.

Eventually a nurse walked over to wake the older girls and let them know about Abby's condition, "Miss Rebecca, your sister is sleeping now, but she's not well at all. I'm surprised your parents allowed it to progress this far before seeking help.

Abigail's terrible cough is deep in her lungs because she has advanced pneumonia. Young children normally fight this sort of thing effectively with our help, but she is quite far along with the sickness. She's so very thin, like we usually see in children who haven't had enough food to eat.

Fortunately, you girls went ahead and brought her in, rather than wait for your parents. That poor little girl might not have lasted the rest of the day. The doctors say they have never seen someone so small with such an awful case. There is nothing more you can do for her, except pray. Now, we must make your parents aware that she is in our care—and may not make it."

Rebecca broke down crying uncontrollably. Marie was crying, too, but came over and wrapped her arms around her friend. This was comforting for Rebecca, and despite her head spinning with thoughts of losing her sister, gave her a little time to think about what she would say to the nurse.

I have to leave Abby with these people and get out of here, she thought. *If they find out we're orphans, Abby might get taken back to the slum dump, and she'll die.*

Rebecca jumped up, took Marie's hand, and pulled her out the door. She yelled back over her shoulder, "I have to tell my father. Please help Abby! We'll be back."

Despite protests behind them, the girls kept running down the hall, past the woman at the table, and out the door. Rebecca glanced both ways, and then motioned to Marie, "Come on, follow me."

They ran down the stairs and around a corner of the hospital where they were able to have a few moments to think about their next move.

"Marie, I'm scared. The nurse said Abby could die, and if we tell them we live at the orphanage, they might send Abby back there, where that mean nurse won't help her. She'll die for sure."

Marie said, "The doctors will help her, Rebecca. We had better get back to the house before they find out we're gone and send us to a detention home. If that happens, even if Abby gets better, you might never see her again."

They both cried and cried, overwhelmed by this adult-sized situation with just two little girls to figure things out. Rebecca was torn about what to do. Should she leave her sister and maybe never see her alive again? Or should she stay and take a chance that all of them would get sent to a detention home? And even if she and Marie could go back to the orphanage and then sneak back to the hospital in a day or two, there was no way they could go through the woods again or take a chance at getting caught on a road or path.

While pondering these terrible choices, Rebecca realized she was including Marie in her life-and-death plans, though she barely knew the girl. She was grateful for Marie's help with her sister, and liked that she was fun and fearless, but also worried about her being too wild and reckless.

She made up her mind, "Marie, we have to get back to the dump."

"Yes, let's hurry," said Marie.

They walked back around the corner to the road. Rebecca took one last, longing look at the hospital. How could she leave her little sister there alone? She fought back another stream of tears, and then said, "All right, Marie, let's g—"

Marie was already ten steps ahead, so Rebecca caught up, and the worn-out girls trudged down the street, concentrating on their feet, so as not to trip on the cobblestones.

7

Marie's Bold Move

The wide road was less busy than it had been earlier, but the girls still had to move aside for the passing carriages. At one point, Rebecca heard the clopping sound of many hooves coming from far behind. The noise kept growing, getting closer and closer, louder and louder, until she and Marie both turned to look.

Rather than horses coming at them, she saw a group of swiftly approaching deer with large sets of horns. The male deer, also called stags, were pulling what looked like an enormous, sparkling, golden carriage that reflected multi-colored sunrays.

Rebecca said, "Is that—? Isn't that Princess Mirra's carriage?"

"What a day," said Marie. "We ran away from the slum dump, survived a dreadful forest, delivered Abby to a hospital, and now, here's the princess."

Rebecca agreed that their day had been extraordinary, but she couldn't get excited like Marie when two horrible worries were bombarding her mind. *Any minute, my sister might die in the hospital, and Marie and I still have to avoid being caught slipping into the orphanage—that is, if the adults don't already know we're gone.*

Marie said, "Maybe the princess is coming from the castle."

"No, the castle is at least a day's ride," said Rebecca, before starting to talk louder to be heard over the thundering hooves. "SHE WAS AT THE SLUM DUMP YESTERDAY. SHE'S PROBABLY BEEN VISITING OTHER TOWNS NEARBY."

Marie asked, "WHERE DO YOU THINK SHE'S GOING?"

Rebecca shrugged.

Marie's face suddenly lit up with her latest, gutsy—and wild—idea, "HEY, LET'S *ASK* HER."

Surprised and terrified, Rebecca protested, "NO! THAT'S A HORRIBLE IDEA! MARIEEEE! DON'T DO THAT!"

But Marie had already taken a couple of steps toward the middle of the street.

Startled by the sight of a child in the road ahead, the coachman quickly pulled back on the reins to slow his team of huge deer.

"What is Marie thinking?" Rebecca whispered to herself, but then she realized it was too late to undo Marie's alarming decision, so she reluctantly went to join her—nervously watching the rapidly-approaching carriage, stags, and royalty.

The massive carriage finally came to a halt a few yards away from Marie. Not bothering to wait for what the coachman or outriders—the mounted assistants who rode beside the carriage—might say, Marie walked up to the carriage's side door, reached up high, and knocked three times.

Rebecca hid her face in her hands. She was embarrassed and scared, but she followed her bold friend in case Marie might need rescuing. A crowd gathered, and tension hung in the air. Everyone waited for whomever might emerge from inside. Soon a high window opened, and Princess Mirra called to her outriders, "Why have we stopped, and who is knocking?"

As Rebecca approached the carriage door, Marie began rambling, "Hi ... uhm, I'm Reb—or ... Marie. This is Rebecca. She ... uh ... we were wondering ... I mean, *just* wondering—so, you can go if you're busy, but if not—if you maybe, could ... I mean, could you maybe ... tell us where you're going?"

When Marie first began talking, Rebecca thought the princess was irritated, but then she looked amused.

"Well, Miss Marie," the princess said, "your bravery is commendable, but why stop us from reaching dinner, just to ask our destination?"

"We were ... I mean ... *are* curious," Marie explained.

Rebecca cringed at the thought of speaking up to help Marie. Much-less-frightening encounters usually made Rebecca speechless, and she still couldn't believe Marie had stopped the royal carriage. But being physically and mentally exhausted, she just wanted the day to be over.

Rebecca said, "What my friend means is that she is asking because we live at the dump ... um ... the orphanage. You visited us yesterday. Well, not just us, but we were there. And you said you would return in three days. We were wondering if you might be back sooner because you are going that way."

Rebecca shrunk back behind Marie, hoping her help might keep them out of the castle dungeon. That really would make their day worse.

The princess replied, "I see, Miss Rebecca. And Miss Marie, I understand your concern. I would not want you to miss my visit, but that will be in a few days, as you correctly mentioned. Now let me ask you a couple of questions. Why are you two not at the children's home, especially since I know you're not allowed in town on your own? And what has gotten you both so filthy?"

Marie said, "We were … umm, just playing … and so we got dirty … and—"

"Your Highness," Rebecca interrupted, knowing Marie's lie was not going to end well, "Thank you for reminding us that we must get back right away—before missing dinner. Unfortunately, we fell into a patch of mud and now we need to wash up before eating. You are most kind to put up with our interruption and question."

Marie opened her mouth, but Rebecca gently kicked her leg, not having the energy left to repair any more problems Marie's mouth might cause. Rebecca started curtsying as she backed away from the carriage. Marie took note and did the same.

Likely guessing the girls were on a harmless adventure, the princess gave them a knowing smile and said, "Though this was an odd encounter, I am glad to have met you both."

The princess signaled her coachman to rouse the deer and all twenty-four hooves sprang into action, stomping and pushing off from the cobblestones with a violent, thunderous noise that caused the carriage to lurch forward and swiftly pull away. From the window, the princess waved to Marie, Rebecca, and the townspeople who had gathered to watch. All of them excitedly returned the wave.

"That could have turned out *much* worse," said Rebecca. "What were you thinking?"

Marie narrowed her eyes a bit and replied, "Why did you interrupt me?"

"I'm so sorry, Marie," said Rebecca, "but I thought of a way to explain why we were away from the dump, and I just hoped she wouldn't offer to take us there."

Marie sighed, nodded in agreement, and changed the subject, "How *are* we going to get back?"

"Well," said Rebecca, "it's probably almost dinnertime, so the adults won't be near the front door. We can probably sneak in now."

With plenty of onlookers, the girls continued through town and into the countryside. Quite a while later, the orphanage came into view. The place had always been depressing when looking at it close up. Now from a distance, the decay and lack of attention was even more obvious. Rebecca thought it reflected their lives at the slum dump—sad, unloved, and falling apart.

The girls had been too tired to talk much on the way back, but then Marie asked a grown-up question, "Rebecca, why do you think God lets some children live in dumps with mean adults, and others get to be princesses living with kings and queens who dearly love them, and probably give them hugs every day?"

Marie's face looked completely different when she was serious. She continued, "Why do only a few girls get to live in beautiful castles with all kinds of animals, and they get to ride on horses or stags and in royal carriages that take them all over the land? And I'm sure Princess Mirra eats wonderful food every day. No wonder she's so nice."

Rebecca was beyond exhausted, but she was amazed at Marie's sincere and thoughtful questions. Rebecca had no immediate answer, so Marie asked again, "If God can do anything, why is He so unfair to you and me?"

Rebecca groaned at the thought of having to think. Her groan matched the sound that her hungry stomach had been making since they left town. Still, Marie's sincere questions had made her wonder about God's plans for people, since He supposedly created everyone. But being too tired for conversation, she half-heartedly replied, "Life is just unfair. Some get everything. Others, nothing."

Unsatisfied, Marie continued, "But can we change it? Why can't you and I and Abby become princesses? Maybe there's a way but we just don't know how. We could be missing out on a wonderful life because we haven't asked anyone."

Then Rebecca heard another dangerous idea from her surprisingly thoughtful friend, "We can ask Princess Mirra," said Marie, "She'll know."

Rebecca shuddered to think of Marie confronting the princess again. She said, "Marie, please, no more trouble. Seriously, you can't go around jumping out at princesses and interrogating them."

By that time, they had reached the slum dump. As expected, it was still dinner time, so no adults were near the front door—outside or in—allowing the girls to sneak home unseen. They even were able to get a portion of flavorless dinner, and then trudge back to their tiny rooms and hard beds.

Rebecca's room felt strange without Abby. Being completely worn out, she quickly fell asleep, but then kept waking, tossing, turning, and temporarily falling back asleep. She had a few nightmares about Abby being at the hospital. When awake, all she could think about was her little sister, as well as Marie's questions.

Marie is right to wonder, Rebecca thought, *Why can't we three be princesses? Why does God allow unpleasant lives for people, especially orphans? Maybe there is no God, which would mean He's not there at the hospital helping Abby. But the doctors are there, and they know what to do. I hope God is also helping. I just don't know. I wish Mother and Father could be here. They would know. But I will pray again, just in case."*

"God," she whispered quietly, "if you are there, please save my sister. She needs help and my parents died, so they aren't with her. I should be there with her at the hospital. But I can't be. Please help the doctors. I *can't* lose Abby! She's all I have left."

Rebecca cried herself back to sleep. Later she woke to conflicting thoughts about her new friend. *Like Abby, Marie is full of fun and cheerful, even with the awful circumstances of our lives. I think Marie could fall in a swamp and probably just get even more excited—maybe at the idea of finding a frog or interesting bug—or maybe even a water snake. How does she keep such a great attitude, while I'm always sad and lonely?*

As Rebecca lay there, she grew to like her new friend more, but then suddenly her thoughts turned dark, maybe influenced by the nightmares. Doubts about Marie began creeping in. *That crazy girl* would *swim after a snake. I'm anxious or annoyed half the time I'm with her. She's way too fearless around people—even princesses. Re-*

becca shook those troubling thoughts out of her mind and resolved to focus on the good in Marie. After all, Marie was the happy one.

She thought, *I am going to help Marie find an answer to her questions about God, even if we have to ask a princess—or swim after a snake.*

With that pledge to focus on helping someone else—as Princess Mirra had suggested in her speech to the orphans—Rebecca gained a bit of peace and was able to sleep the rest of the night without any more dreadful dreams.

8

Out the Window

Rebecca awakened late and missed the morning fruit, but she was thankful for a few hours of sleep. She was relieved that the adults hadn't noticed they had been gone, but also disheartened that nobody had cared enough to check on them—especially since Abby was so sick.

The dreary morning went by slowly without her sister, with more and more worry creeping in as the hours limped by. In an effort to make them go by faster, Rebecca spent the afternoon outdoors with Marie.

Before she'd left her room that day, Rebecca had an idea for something she could make to give Abby upon her return from the hospital. She'd carefully torn off the faces of several of the princes and princesses from the peeling wallpaper. She'd also gathered enough strips of the sapphire blue wallpaper to go with each of the faces.

When Rebecca told Marie her plan, the two girls began collecting wide sticks about eight inches long. Then they looked for sap dripping from trees. Taking a small stick, they scraped it onto a large leaf. The two girls used the sticky substance to attach the prince and princess faces to the top of the sticks. Then they tore the strips of blue wallpaper to fit the remaining space on the wide sticks. That way, each of the princes and princesses would have royally-colored clothing.

While Rebecca finished attaching the pieces, Marie gathered some vines so they could tie belts around the clothing. She even found some small stones that would serve as shoes on the bottom of the sticks once the stones were attached. Even though they weren't anything fancy, Abby would love having her own royal stick puppets to play with on rainy days.

But even staying busy didn't keep the worry about Abby away. Marie did her best to reassure Rebecca that her little sister was probably feeling better. That was a nice thing for her to say, but also annoying, because each hour Rebecca didn't know for *sure* was painful.

Afternoon turned to dusk, dusk to night, and for only the second time in their lives, Rebecca went to bed without hugging Abby. That made her extra sad because she needed hugs as much as Abby did.

Rebecca thought about how Abby had probably asked God extra nicely if He would please give her a dream visit with their parents. That is, if she wasn't too sick to care. For the second night in a row, Rebecca cried herself to sleep.

With little rest the night before, Rebecca slept out of exhaustion, and didn't wake until after breakfast had started. Once she was dressed and out in the hallway, she saw and heard the usual excitement about Princess Mirra visiting that day. Rebecca wished

Abby was there to enjoy it. Rebecca ran downstairs to the dining hall, snatched a piece of fruit, and went to Marie's room.

"There you are," said Marie, "I have an idea."

A jolt of anxiety shot through Rebecca, but she tried to look pleased, so as not to disappoint her friend. Marie motioned her in and Rebecca got her first look at Marie's colossal mess. Heaped around the room lay scattered piles of clothes, bedding, dishes, books, various scraps of things, and her food pile with a couple of half-eaten apples, an unopened banana, a carrot, and a few sticks of rhubarb.

This place is a disaster! thought Rebecca. *I hope the adults don't discover it like this or she'll be in trouble.*

"I was thinking," said Marie, "Princess Mirra is visiting today, and she talks about God, so we can ask her our questions."

Rebecca ignored Marie saying they were "our" questions, especially since Rebecca had vowed to help her friend find answers. She, too, was wondering why life was so unfair. She'd lost her home, her father, her mother, and now—possibly—Abby.

Marie continued, "Princess Mirra is a girl like us, even though she's much older. How old do you think she is?"

Rebecca answered, and then planned to stop the idea she knew Marie was about to tell her. "I think she's maybe eight or ten years older than us—but Marie, we *cannot* talk to her today. She will mention we saw her in town. We'll be in big trouble.

So you *cannot* jump out at her again. Even if we aren't hauled away to the dungeons, I'm sure she won't answer more questions if we rudely spring out at her a second time."

Marie rolled her eyes, "Well, of course we won't surprise her this time. We can wait until she's not with the adults and then just let her see us. She'll remember you and me and want to say hello. It's a foolproof plan. You'll see. It's perfect."

Rebecca returned Marie's eye roll and thought to herself, *We will see. We'll see a disaster—and then the detention home. Apparently, anxiety, alarm, and fear are part of being Marie's friend.* But Rebecca had pledged to help Marie, which meant she had committed to the next wild idea that popped into Marie's head.

Then Rebecca had a much more disturbing thought. *Was an innocent Marie moved away from her past friends, or did her risky ideas cause something horrible to happen to them, so the adults got rid of her? I wonder—*

"BOYS AND GIRLS!" interrupted a man in the first-floor hallway, "NO CHILDREN ARE ALLOWED OUT OF THEIR ROOMS UNTIL AFTER PRINCESS MIRRA'S VISIT."

The two girls looked at each other, Marie with deep disappointment, and Rebecca appearing the same on the outside, while actually being relieved in some ways. She would have liked to have their questions answered, but more than that, she just wanted to know if Abby was any better. Still, she was glad that Marie wouldn't be jumping out at Princess Mirra again.

But Rebecca's short-lived peace shattered when another wild idea struck inside Marie's mind. Springing to her feet, Marie pushed a stool to the wall. Then she jumped up on it, unlatched and opened the window, and put her legs over the windowsill to climb out.

"Marie! What are you doing?"

Rebecca was astonished back into silence when Marie twisted sideways and sort of jumped and rolled off the window ledge.

"Marie!" Rebecca yelled somewhat softly, while thinking, *This was* not *her first time doing that.*

"Come on," said Marie from outside. "You're next. Hurry."

Not a risk taker, Rebecca had never had a serious injury, but she suspected Marie might have had several broken bones from the reckless way she flings herself about. The cautious sister reluctantly got onto the stool and stood, relieved to see the shrubs that had broken Marie's fall. Rebecca hesitantly crawled out onto the ledge, stretched a leg out to reach the bush, eased off the windowsill—and fell—disappearing into the shrubbery. Marie reached in to help Rebecca climb out.

"Marie," said Rebecca, still tangled in a bush and looking up from the ground, "Next time, can you please tell me the plan before we go?"

"I'm sorry," said Marie, "but we have to catch Princess Mirra as she arrives. Now let's hurry and find the right place hide behind the shrubs."

The girls ducked down between the wall and bushes, mostly out of sight. Then Marie motioned for Rebecca to follow her as she began crawling toward the corner of the building that turned to the front door.

Once there, Marie peered around and reported back, "Oh, no. She's already here."

"Let's hurry back inside," said Rebecca, though she wondered *how* they would get back up to the window.

"No," said Marie, "we just have to wait until she leaves."

Reluctantly, Rebecca agreed. The two sat behind the bushes for a long, long while, waiting for the princess's carriage to leave the front of the building and turn down the road onto the side where they were waiting.

Having a few moments to think, Rebecca suddenly realized her friend's plan, something that filled her with horror.

"Marie," she whispered, "You're going to jump out at her again, aren't you?"

Marie's excited smile was her answer. The wary sister sighed, deciding to continue waiting with Marie in the bushes. Marie was going to need a friend to break her out of the castle dungeon. Rebecca shook her head in despair. If anyone had told her a year ago that she'd be in this position, she wouldn't have believed them. But here she was.

Quite a while later, both heard a commotion around the corner. "It's time," whispered Marie ... well, at least as much of a whisper as Marie could achieve.

Rebecca looked out to the road and said, "They will be going slowly around the corner, so you'll have to catch them before—"

Leaving no possibility of missing them, Marie had already bolted from the bushes and was taking long strides toward the road. Rebecca remained in hiding, watching as Marie took her position, blocking Princess Mirra's path. There she stood while Rebecca began to feel guilty for not being there to help her friend.

Rounding the corner, the coachman must have recognized the familiar sight in the road. The stags and carriage came to a halt. An outrider jumped down and retrieved a set of steps from the back of the carriage. He placed them on the ground for the princess, knocked twice on her door, paused, and then knocked twice more.

Soon the door opened, and the princess slowly descended the steps as she took a quick look around. Spotting Marie, she walked to the front of the deer. "Ooohhh, myyy." said Princess Mirra.

Rebecca couldn't tell if the princess was angry, but she thought she better join her friend—regardless of the consequences.

"There you are again, Miss Marie. And once more I see Miss Rebecca following behind. Two days ago, you two were in town when you should have been here, and now, you're outside when you should be inside. Have you been granted a special pass for excellent behavior, or perhaps you don't live here at all and you're really just the curious children of a forest family?"

"We *do* live here," said Marie, "And we *are* supposed to be in our rooms—"

"Then your answer," interrupted the princess, "should address why neither of you are presently inside."

She's definitely annoyed, thought Rebecca, as she reached Marie.

"We crawled out a window," said Marie.

Rebecca was astonished at her friend's complete honesty and braced for whatever might be Princess Mirra's reaction to this surprising confession. But she only seemed intrigued.

"Well, it seems you're honest," said the Princess. "Now, before I turn you over to your caretakers, for what important reason have you halted our carriage this time?"

9

A Grand Idea

Rebecca decided she would take the lead from now on whenever she and Marie were with royalty.

Marie answered Princess Mirra's question with a question about whether it was okay to ask questions, "Your Royal Highness, I … or … umm … we were wondering if, because you're also a girl like us, can we ask you something important?"

"Yes, you may," agreed the Princess, "but first, girl to girls, let me ask you something. Is Miss Rebecca onboard with these adventures, or are you the ringleader who gets reluctant friends in trouble with you?"

Marie seemed stumped for an answer and Rebecca recognized that the princess was probably right about Marie getting friends in trouble. But Rebecca decided this was the time to start supporting her anyway.

"She is a good friend," said Rebecca, "and I want to help her."

Looking a little amused, the princess replied, "I'm glad you're a team. Now, my entourage has far to travel this day, so please ask your question directly, plainly, and quickly."

Marie looked at Rebecca, indicating she should answer.

"Thank you, Princess Mirra. We're wondering if you know why God gives some children amazing lives, while others have terrible things happen to them every day, like having to live in a slum dump with no father or mother."

Rebecca felt terrible at the realization that she had characterized their home as a dump. Her anxiety rose as the princess remained silent for what felt like a whole minute. Just before Rebecca was going to speak up and apologize, royal Mirra took Marie's habit of hatching ideas to a new level, "You bold and curious girls deserve the best answer to your crucial question about life. It's one *I* could address satisfactorily; however, I know someone who can explain better."

Looking right at Marie, she added, "How would you like to go on an amazing journey?"

Marie nodded her head so fast and so many times that Rebecca wondered how she didn't become dizzy and fall down.

The princess continued, "Though, I'll warn you, we can't have you popping out at people on the road."

They all laughed, and then Rebecca asked, "On the *road?*"

Princess Mirra continued, "Our wise King Mesharet gained his great knowledge under the King of kings." She paused, a smile spreading across her face. "How would you girls like to meet my father?"

Rebecca gasped in disbelief. Marie spouted gibberish: "Wha—your ... when ... ya ... woah!"

The princess laughed while they collected themselves. Finally, Marie asked, "Can we? Truly? When?"

Mirra took Marie's excitement for at least one yes, so she motioned her into the carriage. Marie ran to the stairs where an outrider put out his hand to help her, but she jumped up the steps by herself and disappeared inside.

Mirra turned to Rebecca, who suddenly had tears running down her face. The alarmed princess approached her, put a hand on her shoulder, and asked, "Are you alright, Rebecca?"

"I'm sorry, Your Highness," she replied, "I want to go but there is a huge, horrible problem. My little sister, Abigail, is in the hospital and she's very, very sick—" Rebecca broke down sobbing and couldn't continue. The Princess knelt down—with no concern for her elegant dress—and wrapped her arms around the orphan. That made Rebecca cry even harder. Other than from Abby, this was the first hug she'd had since her parents had died.

When she was able, Rebecca continued through sobs, "I ... don't know ... if ... Abby is alive."

When Rebecca hadn't followed her into the carriage, Marie came back, arriving in time to help Rebecca explain. "Princess Mirra, we had to take Abby to a doctor because the orphanage nurse wouldn't help her. We left home, went through an awful forest, walked into town, and left Abby at the hospital because Rebecca and I had to get back to the orphanage before we were caught and sent to a detention home."

"I see, so that's why you were in town by yourselves. How old is Miss Abigail?

"She's only four," said a now-more-composed Rebecca. "She was terribly sick with pneumonia, but we had to leave the hospital quickly while she was sleeping, so I didn't even get to say goodbye. If she's even okay, I know she must be scared without me, wondering where I went, and when I'll be back. I'm all she has now that Mother and Father are gone."

Still with an arm around Rebecca, and now with deep concern on her face, Princess Mirra thought for a few minutes. She then offered her solution, "Unfortunately, we must leave now and we're going the opposite direction from town. But if you agree, I have a plan. First, we three girls, the coachman, and the outriders will gather and pray for God's help in healing your precious sister. Then with two of our stags, I will send two of our swiftest riders to find Miss Abigail. They will let her know your whereabouts, assess her health, and bring her to us—*if* she is fit to travel.

"Having only four stags pulling this huge carriage will slow us down, which is why we must leave right away, but two outriders on two stags will be fast. They will catch us on the road at some point. Once we reach the castle, Miss Abigail will be seen by the top doctors in the land."

The princess paused, held Rebecca tighter, and continued in a soft, slow tone, "At the hospital in town, if the riders find a troubling situation with your sister—of any kind—one will remain with her, and the other will dash back to us and deliver the news."

This plan gave Rebecca some relief, but her terrified mind would have her on the edge of breaking down until she knew Abby was okay. Princess Mirra called over a couple of the outriders. They unhitched two deer from the carriage, saddled them, and then the riders raced off down the road.

Princess Mirra turned to Rebecca again, "Now, Miss Abigail has the help of this entire kingdom, while we three have a long trip ahead. If I am even five minutes late at the castle, my parents will have everyone in the land looking for us."

Rebecca nodded and the princess turned toward the carriage steps. An outrider opened the door and Marie shot past the other two, leaping up the stairs and—this time—*jumping* in. In a distraught and stunned haze, Rebecca followed Mirra up the stairs and through the door, where the first thing Rebecca noticed were all the pillows. She thought, *No wonder Marie flung herself inside.*

When the princess and Rebecca were seated, with Marie lying in the pillows, Mirra motioned out the window and the coachman yelled to his massive deer, "Yaw! Yaw!" Even having lost a third of their team, the four majestic stags sprang forward and quickly made it to a gallop. Rebecca and Marie peered out the back window and watched the roof of their cheerless home get smaller and smaller, until it soon disappeared.

In the extravagant back room of the carriage, Princess Mirra sat with Rebecca and Marie. Both girls gazed in awe at the scarlet and emerald interior, gold fixtures, and dark, polished wood. The princess had the high bench, opposite where Rebecca and Marie sat on the low bench below the back window.

Besides having thick, plush blankets, Rebecca guessed the room had over a dozen of the softest pillows ever made. She stroked her hand across the silky surfaces, soaking in the almost-forgotten feeling of comfort. Everything at the orphanage was rough, including their pillows, mattresses, food, and the way they were treated.

The entire carriage was a level of luxury Rebecca had never daydreamed about, even through the countless days spent staring at the tattered royal wallpaper, thinking about just this sort of life. For a while she and Marie were speechless—yes, even Marie. But when the shock wore off enough, Marie asked Mirra, "Your Highness, why did you let us in here?"

Mirra tilted her head and showed slight concern, "Well, Miss Marie, you are full of questions—which is wonderful—but are you implying I made a mistake?"

"Yes!" said Marie. "I mean … no, no mistake."

Rebecca added, "But as busy as you must be, why did you decide to help a couple of orphans in such a huge way?"

The princess said, "*Everyone,* child or adult, deserves to know their life's purpose. You specifically asked to learn more about yours, so I want to help you find answers."

Both girls nodded and smiled, but Rebecca wasn't sure what fairness had to do with her life's purpose. She contemplated Mirra's answer for the next couple of hours while peering out the windows, marveling at the beautiful countryside. Hills, valleys, forests, farms, towns, people, and animals all passed before the girls' wondering eyes.

Hours into the journey, Princess Mirra raised her head from the scrolls she had been reading and marking. "You two must be hungry," she said. "I have quick business where we will stop for an afternoon meal at an inn."

As they soon passed through a small town, the carriage stopped in front of an elegant, old building. The princess opened the carriage door and stepped down to the ground, followed by the other two.

Walking inside the building, Rebecca was struck by the scent of baking bread. She hadn't smelled that wonderful aroma since her mother was alive. The staff served people at long tables covered with tablecloths, large vases of colorful flowers, goblets, pitchers of water, and salt cellars (salt-filled containers that served as the centerpiece of the table). Only the wealthy had salt since it cost so much, which meant this would be a real treat for the girls.

Besides some natural light, the room was filled with flickering candles on the tables and in iron fixtures hanging from the ceiling. Beautiful tapestries and paintings covered the walls.

Once Rebecca and Marie were seated in a large, private recess at the back wall, waiters brought fruit-flavored drinks and assorted delicacies. First came a heavenly chicken soup, and then ripe, brightly colored fruits for dipping in melted chocolate, as well as fresh vegetables with tasty sauces. Following this were large cuts of spiced meats placed in thick slices of warm bread—fresh out of the oven—making sandwiches so thick the girls could not open their mouths wide enough to take a bite.

Back from her business with the owner, Mirra saw her new friends struggling and motioned for the head waiter, who quickly came over and cut their food into manageable pieces. The girls ate and ate, especially from the pastry tower of delightful sweet macarons that were served at the end of the meal. Rebecca marveled at how flavorful everything was. She'd forgotten how good food could taste after several years of eating aged rhubarb, dry overcooked rabbit, and bland stews.

Rebecca ate to the point of worrying that she might get ill on the carriage ride. Finally, she stopped eating and waited for the other two to finish. Walking out, they each thanked the staff—the orphans did so too many times, but they were quite grateful for the delicious food and all the wonderful treatment.

Getting back into the carriage, Rebecca and Marie plopped down on the pillows, as Princess Mirra sat properly on her soft bench. Not long into the carriage moving again, the younger girls became quite tired from having just eaten the largest meal of their lives.

"You two might like a nap," said the princess. "After the nearby mountain pass, we'll be deep into forest for a while, so you won't see much." She turned to Rebecca, "And I'm sure you could use a break from worrying about Miss Abigail."

Rebecca slept until evening and then lay there a while with her eyes closed, listening to the trotting stags and the jostling of the carriage. She didn't want to fully wake up in case this was all a big dream. But as reality returned to her still-sleepy brain, she suddenly opened her eyes and looked over at the princess who was studying her papers. "Excuse me, Your Royal Highness?"

"Yes?"

"We have not properly thanked you," said Rebecca. "I want to say thank you *so, so much* for helping us—especially Abby."

"You are welcome," said the princess, "and I know we will soon get word of your precious sister. I am overjoyed to have you and excitable Marie along. Trips alone can be quite boring. Besides, both of your questions get to the core of our lives." Mirra picked up and held out a scroll, "Wouldn't it be grand if our Creator gave us some writing—like a scroll or book—that has every instruction we need for a wonderful life?"

"Yes, it would," agreed Rebecca, while Marie remained sprawled out across the pillows, sleeping soundly as the two girls continued their conversation.

The princess said, "Well, you will soon find out that God did exactly that. My heartfelt desire is that every boy or girl around the world would learn this. Our kingdom's help is for anyone who asks. This trip is because you and Marie boldly made known your search for answers. Well, Marie mostly did, and your reward is for supporting a friend."

Rebecca nodded as Mirra leaned forward and added, "From the first moment we girls met in town, something told me we would be friends."

Shocked that an actual princess just called her a friend, Rebecca could only nod and squeak out, "Ya … es."

Mirra leaned back, "And speaking of friendship, I would love to know your full names."

Rebecca could not remember the last time she mentioned her middle name. "Rebecca Findley Faith," she said, and then suddenly realized she didn't know Marie's full name, even though they had talked quite a bit. She glanced at Marie and made a suggestion. "Princess Mirra, maybe we should wait to talk about names with Marie. I know she wouldn't want to miss it."

Yes, quite so," said Mirra. "Why don't we both follow her lead and get more sleep? At night the deep woods have little light, leaving nothing to see but a few stars now and then through the treetops."

With that, the princess stretched out on her bench, covering up with a velvety blanket. Rebecca closed her eyes for quite a while but couldn't sleep. Eventually growing tired of trying to be tired, she opened her eyes, sat up, and noticed that Princess Mirra was gone. Then she saw that Marie was somewhat awake and looking over at her.

"Where's Princess Mirra?" whispered Rebecca.

"I guess she went to the front compartment," said Marie, speaking loudly.

Rebecca cringed a bit and then again demonstrated whispering, hoping her loud friend would take the hint, "Marie, I have not asked your full name."

"Oh … umm … well …" Marie said more quietly, but then turned away before finishing her answer. When she looked back a few moments later, light reflecting from one of the small lanterns revealed tears in her eyes. This time Marie spoke slowly and softly, "I don't know my full name. I know nothing of my parents, and I have no idea where I'm from."

"Oh, I am *so* sorry, Marie," said Rebecca. She thought about it for a few moments and added, "You know though, who you are *now* is most important, and from what I've learned about you so far, you're a fun, brave, kind, and loyal friend."

"Thank you, Becky," said Marie. "You are a wonderful friend too. You've been patient with me … and nice … and supportive. And you don't tell me I annoy you, though I know I do."

Both girls reached out to each other, had a long warm embrace, and then settled back where they were.

Rebecca thought, *Marie's right. She does annoy me some, but that doesn't matter as much as her good qualities. That must be so sad for Marie to not have any memories of her mother and father, or to not know what town she came from, or even her full name.*

The girls sat for a while looking out the carriage windows, watching flashes of the moon and tiny stars going by between the trees. Eventually Marie tipped over into the pillows and went back to sleep. Rebecca sighed and continued sitting, knowing she would probably not sleep again until she knew Abby was okay.

10

The Outrider Returns

Eventually Rebecca felt the driver slowing the stags and they soon stopped. Out the back window was a long, straight road lit by a full moon. Far off in the distance, Rebecca thought she could see something coming, something tiny but growing.

She whispered to herself, "Is it the stags? Maybe there's news about Abby!"

Rebecca jumped up, opened the door quickly, held on to some metal ornamentation on the side of the carriage, and then dropped to the ground.

She ran to the front and asked the coachman, "Sir, why have we stopped?"

He replied, "Briefly resting the stags, miss."

Rebecca ran back to the rear of the carriage and confirmed that whatever it was in the distance was still growing. *The princess said we would see both outriders and stags if Abby was able to come with them.*

She intensely watched down the dimly-lit road, and soon it looked like at least one large animal. *But is there another behind that one?* Her stomach churned with nerves.

To get a better look, she turned to the carriage, climbed up the luggage, and stood at the top, squinting and straining to see a second figure that would confirm Abby was alive. She wanted to look, but was also afraid to. Because at that moment for Rebecca, a joyful or wrecked life depended on seeing two deer and two riders, one of whom would be carrying a beautiful, brown-haired little girl. Rebecca's heart felt like it had jumped to her throat.

The moving image grew larger until Rebecca realized it really was a stag, and soon she could see the head and shoulders of a man.

"It's them! It's them!" she shouted.

This celebration roused the carriage passengers. But Rebecca's joy combined with paralyzing fear as she waited for the entire picture to become clear. And then she knew ... there was one stag, one rider ... and no little girl. Rebecca fell on the luggage and wailed. Questions shot through her mind, *Where's the other rider? What happened at the hospital? Oh, how could I have left her there alone? Is she dead? She must be, if she isn't with them! Why would God take my whole family? Why?*

By this time, the coachman had placed the stairs under the door, allowing Mirra and Marie to come out and hear Rebecca's distress. They went to the back and saw her there on the luggage, crying.

They helped her down and both girls wrapped their arms around her. Sobbing inconsolably, Rebecca struggled to get the words out, "There's ... only ... one rider. Abby ... must ... be dead."

With tears in her eyes, Princess Mirra tried to console Rebecca while Marie watched the lone rider coming closer. Apparently noticing something strange, Marie yelled, "Look! What's that?"

Rebecca looked up. The outrider was close enough that she could recognize his bearded face. Then she saw what Marie had probably seen. Through the tears glazing Rebecca's vision, she focused on movement behind his back on both sides. Soon it became clear. They were hands—very small hands—her little sister's hands!

"Abby! Oh, Abby!" shouted Rebecca.

A little brown-haired head peeked around the rider's back. "Becky! Becky!"

Marie said, "It's her. She's alive! Abby's back!"

Rebecca ran to meet the stag and rider as Princess Mirra, Marie, the coachman, and the other outriders celebrated.

When Rebecca got close enough, the man stopped his stag and Abby leaned toward her sister, stretching out an arm and revealing the harness on the outrider's back, the one that had kept her safe from falling off the giant deer. He undid the contraption, then lowered a still-harnessed Abby down to her sister.

They enjoyed a long embrace. Rebecca didn't want to ever let her go again. Eventually, Rebecca said, "Abby, I am *so* sorry I left you at the hospital, but you were asleep and that was where you had to go to get better. Marie and I needed to get back to the dump before they found out we were gone. Otherwise, they could have sent us to a detention home without you. I promise never to leave you again. I was *so* worried. I thought you died! Are you okay now?"

"Yes, I'm better," said Abby. Her words came out in a rush, "They gave me wonderful things to eat. I didn't know food could taste so good! The bed was so soft and the nurses were kind to me. But the medicine was tewwible." She made a funny face that had all of them laughing. Abby continued, "And then I got to ride on a really fast deer with my new friend who came to get me."

Rebecca smiled at her sister and then looked up at the man, "Sir, I can never thank you enough. But where is the other rider?"

In a deep, booming voice, the broad-shouldered man who had brought Abby home said, "After hearing your desperate story of all you went through so your sister could get to the hospital, we asked the doctors about the severity of Abby's condition when you and Miss Marie brought her in.

"They reported the sad shape she was in and how she could have died—yet no help was given at the children's home. Hearing this, the other outrider left immediately to go rid the orphanage of that terrible nurse. The kingdom will be charging the home with endangering a child."

"Thank you, sir," said Rebecca. "And you're so kind to bring her safely back to me."

Rebecca turned to her little sister, "Did the men tell you who we are traveling with?"

"Yes! The pwincess!" replied Abby. Pointing at the carriage she added, "And it's true—she's wight there. She's so beautiful."

"Do you want to meet her?" asked Rebecca.

"I sure do," Abby replied, but she seemed a bit shy about actually speaking to the princess.

"Why don't you run and give her a hug?" said Rebecca.

Abby took off running down the road toward the princess. Mirra pulled Abby up into a warm embrace, and then Marie wrapped her arms around both of them.

The princess said, "We are overjoyed to see you, Miss Abigail. We were all dreadfully worried about you."

"Abby, I'm so happy you're okay," said Marie.

With tears in her eyes, Abby said, "Marie, thank you for going with Rebecca to get me to the hospital. You helped save me."

Still in the princess's arms, Abby looked up at the spacious, blue, white, and golden carriage, her eyes huge. "Do we get to ride in *that?*" she asked.

"You're not going to believe it, Abby. We're on our way to see the king!" squealed Marie.

"YAY!" Abby shouted.

Rebecca thought about the sudden change in her and Abby's lives. *Just recently, we had no friends, Abby was deathly ill, and a few improvements at the dump were our only hope for a better life. Now Abby's back and feeling much better. We have our great new friends Marie and Mirra—a princess no less—and we're on a wonderful journey in a golden carriage, on our way to see the king.*

I'm living in one of those fairy tales I dreamed about. She gasped as she realized something. *No, this is way better than a fairy tale. Because God truly answered that prayer where I asked him to send someone to care about us. And now, he's sent me on my quest—a journey to learn more about God.*

But while she was enjoying the happiness of that moment, a familiar darkness struck. *Now I know what losing Abby would really feel like,* she thought, *so I can't give her the whole story of what happened with the fire and our parents' death. I will* never *tell her because then she might hate me and I'd be alone in the world.*

Princess Mirra let Abby down from their hug. She commanded that the outrider's deer be rejoined with the carriage. Then she gave the signal to depart. One of the men lifted Abby inside and the other girls followed. Soon the carriage was speeding down the road. Abby fell asleep right away. She was still tired from being sick, and the bouncing of the stag had kept her awake as they rode to meet Rebecca, Marie, and the princess. Soon the older, exhausted girls slept as well.

They traveled through the rest of that night and into the first light of the morning. When Marie woke, her usual noisiness roused the rest. The girls were delighted when Princess Mirra opened a large basket with tea, biscuits, and fruit—without wrinkles or spots. They each ate their fill while looking out at the beautiful scenery passing by. After the sun had climbed high in the sky, Rebecca was the first to spot their destination on the horizon, "Look! Is that the castle?" she asked in awe.

Princess Mirra replied, "Yes, and just wait until we get even closer. It really is the size of a mountain."

A bit later the carriage topped a high hill and the girls could see the entire, gargantuan castle. It dwarfed the town below, but they could soon make out what looked like a church, a few shops, the market, and a huge lake. Getting closer, they saw all kinds of activity with people and animals everywhere. Abby's head swiveled back and forth and back and forth. She'd been at the orphanage since she was tiny, so all of this had to be like a dream—especially the castle.

Rebecca marveled at the lush, green land, full of tall trees, with a fast-flowing river that twisted along until she could see it going beneath the bridge to the castle. They soon passed by a fortress gate where guards stood at attention. The team of stags pulled the carriage around a high, circular road, leading to a turn that would take them down a lane that crossed the bridge into the castle.

Blanketing the landscape on both sides of the road were thousands of colorful, flowering plants. Abby pointed, "Rebecca, look at all the colors. I didn't know flowers smelled pretty like that." A magnificent fountain shot plumes of water from an enormous red and gold cross made of marble. Rebecca would have loved to just sit there for a while and listen to the sound of the water.

Once across the bridge, the carriage actually stopped inside the castle, where light coming from windows and openings above on all sides lit a long courtyard that led to an inner castle door. The princess exited the carriage first, and the other three followed her down the stairs. Abby's legs were a little short for the steps—and she was still weak—so the coachman stepped forward with a smile and a courtly bow and helped her down—just like she was royalty.

The princess led them through perfectly shaped hedges surrounding flower gardens with everything laid out in stunning patterns. Rebecca's eyes darted around, trying to take it all in. She wondered if these sights and smells might be what their mother and father were experiencing in heaven. Workers with carts, oxen, and horses transported equipment, hay, timber, and other supplies, as well as baskets of grains, fruits, and vegetables. All the activity was almost dizzying after their dull life at the orphanage.

Through a few openings in the hedges, Rebecca could see knights training with swords and spears. Near the knights were high-backed, dark-wood chairs where a few royally dressed, grey-bearded noblemen sat.

At the end of the courtyard the four girls approached two towering, silver doors.

Abby tugged on Rebecca's dress and whispered nervously, "How do we get in?"

Of course, Marie had no fears, so she ran ahead and knocked, making Princess Mirra laugh. Overwhelmed, Rebecca said nothing, feeling so undeserving to be meeting a king.

11

The King of Kings

The gigantic doors seemed to open on their own and the girls walked into the entry hall. The walls stretched way, way up to what appeared to be an open ceiling showing the night sky. But Rebecca knew it was the middle of the day, so she realized a realistic full moon and stars had been painted there.

Marie turned to Rebecca and Abby, "We could fly kites in here."

Rebecca noticed the indoor wind as the princess said, "Yes, Marie, this fortress is so mountainous that it has a steady, cool breeze blowing through, even when it's blazing hot outdoors. And during cooler seasons, with the help of the wind, we keep dozens of fireplaces burning."

Next, they entered a cavernous hall. Rebecca thought the entire kingdom could probably dine there together at the same time. They walked on a red and purple carpet that stretched down the center of the room, leading to another broad set of silver doors, but this time they had gold trim and were smaller than the first ones they had gone through, though still quite impressive.

Stationed in front of the doors were two intimidating knights. As the girls drew closer to the men, Rebecca thought they looked even more frightening, so she stopped. Almost immediately Marie bumped her from behind and set her into motion again. Marie was looking everywhere around the room except in front of her. Princess Mirra confidently approached the doors, and they were so heavy that it took both knights to open one side.

Inside the doors, the orphans halted in amazement at the magnificent throne made of solid gold, with a majestic, powerful-looking man sitting on it—King Mesharet. His dark hair flowed over broad shoulders, providing the frame for a long, bushy beard with steaks of grey. His royal blue and white robe was as beautiful to look at as the gleaming, golden crown on his head.

Rebecca thought, *He easily fills that enormous chair—and even sits like a king.*

Coming closer she noticed his royal seat had dark-wood sides encrusted with lines of silver, bright diamonds, rich red rubies, deep-blue sapphires, and sparkling green emeralds. Awestruck and a bit frightened, Rebecca watched Princess Mirra walk boldly to her father. He stood, hugged her warmly, and they talked quietly for a few moments.

She backed away, bowed low, and then rose to formally address the king, speaking in a clear, strong tone, "Your Majesty, may I introduce Miss Rebecca, Miss Marie, and Miss Abigail. They seek answers to important matters."

Princess Mirra stepped aside and the king addressed the orphans, "Please," he said in a booming voice, "Come forward."

The hug he had given his daughter helped Rebecca feel better about approaching him. She walked closer and curtsied, noticing the king's striking, cobalt-blue eyes. Marie and Abby followed. King Mesharet looked at each of their faces and then said, "If Queen Narissa weren't away, she would have enjoyed meeting you three lovely young ladies."

Looking at Abby he added, "And Miss Abigail, she would be quite concerned about your illness. How are you feeling, little lady?"

"Better," said Abby, "No more hurty cough."

Leaning forward, he looked at the two older girls and said, "Our outrider rid your orphanage of its terrible medical staff. I'm so sorry for the unforgivable neglect of Miss Abigail. Praise God that you brave girls were able to take matters into your own hands.

The outrider found orphanage records about you three. He cut through the mountains to come straight here and report to me. Then I had the kingdom scholars look at the history of your families. I'm sure you'll find what they discovered quite interesting."

He leaned back, "How was your trip?"

Uncharacteristically, Marie stood silent so Rebecca said, "Your Highness, Princess Mirra has been extremely kind to us. Once I got Abby back, the journey was the most amazing time of our lives."

The king smiled. "Miss Marie," he said, "You became an orphan before your first birthday. Do you know anything about your family?"

Marie stared for a few moments, looking somewhat ashamed, and then shook her head. The king continued, "You were born to

Jonah and Elizabeth McKenna. They named you Marie Rose. When you were only eleven months old, your parents had to leave you in the care of neighbors so they could travel to help family who lived far away. On their way home to you, they died on a mountain road in a terrible winter storm. The neighbors were too old to raise a child, so they brought you to an orphanage."

Marie sat and wept for a minute until the king supplied much-needed hope. "Marie," he said, "despite that tragedy, there is some seemingly wonderful news. It appears Jonah and Elizabeth were godly people. I cannot know for sure if they *believed in their hearts* that Jesus is their Savior. I cannot know whether they *said so* with their mouths, but from learning about their faith, I believe they did. If true, this means they are waiting in heaven to see you again. You only need to choose heaven as they did."

Rebecca and Abby put their arms around Marie and she cried a while longer. When her tears were gone, her only question was, "How do I *choose* heaven? Of course I will!"

The king replied, "Bless you, Miss Marie, but you can't choose without knowing your choices, so we will talk about that. First, I want to give the sisters their family history."

Extreme fear struck Rebecca as the king continued, "Though Miss Rebecca knows some of this, and I'm sure she's told Abby, maybe we can add some details."

The others must have noticed the shock and sorrow on Rebecca's face before she sat down and put her head in her hands. Memories of the night their family's house burnt down raced through Rebecca's mind. Before the king started to share the details, she felt she had to tell her sister the whole truth. Though relieved to finally confess, she was terrified that Abby would hate her for causing the death of their parents.

Looking at her beloved little sister, she began the awful story she had replayed in her mind countless times. "Abby," she said, "I have a terrible secret I have kept from you, one that I should have told you long ago, but I've been afraid you'd never want to talk to me again. I can't lose you too!"

"Becky, it's okay," said Abby. "Nothing would ever make me stop loving you. You're the best sister ever."

Though unconvinced that she would feel the same way when the truth was told, Rebecca began retelling the horrible events of that night, "Abby, you don't remember because you stayed asleep, but we were all sleeping when Rusty's barking woke us up. Do you remember Rusty? He was our dog.

"The house was smoky. Mother pointed to flames at the far end of the house, and Father picked you up from the bed. He said you had breathed too much smoke. We all ran outside through the back door. They put you on the grass and made sure you were okay before father started to go back into the house. But then he didn't, maybe because he thought there was already too much fire."

Beginning to sob, Rebecca struggled to continue, "That's when … I … I remembered Rusty. I thought I heard him barking at the front of the house. Abby, I had … to … go get him. We both loved Rusty. I ran around to the front and went in the door. The fire was loud and scary. I shouted for Mother and Father, and when I did, Rusty ran to me. That's when I saw our parents come in the back door. They were yelling at me to run out the front door, and it was … it was … the last time I … I ever saw them.

Almost finished, Rebecca felt relief to finally tell the whole truth, "I ran out like they told me, and as I did, the roof came crashing down. Abby, I took off around the house to the backyard and picked you up. We waited and waited … but Mother and Father … never came out."

Relieved that her secret was out, Rebecca lowered her head and waited for the consequences. King Mesharet left his throne, and along with Princess Mirra, they joined the others who were comforting Rebecca. His arms reached around all of them.

Underneath it all, Rebecca heard Abby quietly say, "Becky, I still love you."

Rebecca smiled in relief, overjoyed to hear those words.

After everyone embraced a bit longer, the king went back to his chair and the other girls sat around Rebecca, even the princess.

"Miss Rebecca," said King Mesharet, "you are a brave girl who loved her parents and her dog. You could not have known the mistake you made when trying to save your furry friend from the fire.

We flawed humans make mistakes and hurt others throughout our lives, but we must continue loving each other, just as God looks past our failures and bad behavior. Our Lord goes on loving us no matter what we do, which is the example we need to follow. You and Abby will always be loving sisters."

The king looked at Abby and then Marie, "Now let's talk about how each of you can again be with your mother and father one day. Besides Marie's godly father and mother, I have been told that Rebecca and Abby's parents were also Christians—so you three have royal parents."

What! Royal parents? Rebecca couldn't believe it.

The king continued, "But first, please ask the questions you came to ask, after which I will have one to ask each of you."

Having turned to Rebecca as he finished, she realized he meant for her to answer. She was immediately nervous again, so she took a couple of deep breaths and blurted out all she and Marie had talked about. "Marie first came up with these, but we are wondering why horrible things happen if God can do anything. And though Princess Mirra is such a kind and magnificent friend, how come girls like her get to live a royal life with loving parents, while others like us have to stay in awful places with no parents and mean adults?"

The king paused for a few moments and then said, "Miss Marie, you came up with important questions. And Miss Rebecca, you asked them well. In fact, men, women, boys, and girls have debated them for centuries, even though God gave us the answers long ago."

The orphans sat listening in amazement at the wise king.

12

Liars and Thieves

King Mesharet continued, "Now, please understand that God created and owns everything and everyone. He is my King, your King, and the King of all who have ever lived—*the King of kings!* Queen Narissa and Princess Mirra are princesses in God's kingdom. For now, God allows me to rule this area as His prince, which means I am just an earthly king. God is the King of all kings.

"As far as what God says about life being unfair and bad things happening, your answers can be found in His Word, the Bible, the only book that contains our world history from the Creator of the universe Who was there for it all. It also gives us His instructions for a joyful life and the way we can get to heaven—where we can live for eternity with our Heavenly Father—if we so choose. Later, I'll give each of you a Bible so you can read it for yourselves and grow in wisdom, just as Princess Mirra has.

"God makes each of us one-of-a-kind. He made you young ladies exactly who He wanted you to be, inside and out. Then during your entire lives, though you couldn't see Him, God has always been by your side, causing everything that happens to you to turn out for your own good.

"Such as how Abby's unfortunate hospital stay led to Rebecca and Marie meeting Mirra and eventually coming here today. Yes, we will all have difficult times, because this is a hard world, but God helps us learn from those struggles. Do you understand so far?"

"Yes," said Marie, "But why *is* life so hard?"

"Well, Miss Marie, God made us a wonderful, beautiful world that was perfectly fair and had absolutely *no* hardship. He also created the first person, Adam, and gave him and future generations the planet. Can you imagine being given the entire earth? Then God made Adam a wife named Eve. After giving them all of that, the Creator had only one simple rule: They could eat anything in the world except the fruit from just one tree. That should have been an easy law to follow, right?"

"Yes, it sure should have been," said Rebecca, "but I know the story and they did eat from the forbidden tree. After all God did for them, why would they do that to Him?"

"Great question," said the king. "Let me ask you another question. If you could create people, would you *make* them to like you, or would you *ask* them like you?"

"I don't know, said Rebecca. "It would be nice if they liked me."

"Yes, you would hope so, but if you made them like you—or even made them love you—how could you ever know if they really wanted to be your friend? They might only act like your friend because you forced them to. Would you give your people the choice of who they like and love?"

"Yes, I would."

"Well, that's what God did with Adam and Eve. He gave every human the free will to like and love Him—or not … to obey Him—or not. And even whether to have any kind of relationship with Him at all. Forcing someone to love you is not real love. But either way, the Creator can set rules if He wants, and, unfortunately, Adam and Eve used their free choice to disobey God's only rule.

"They were talked into it by the inventor of rule-breaking, the devil. You see, even before God created our world and us, He made angels in heaven, and He also gave them the free will to break God's rules. Satan, the devil, was the first to use that freedom to break God's rules, which the Bible calls sinning.

"Then after our world was made, the inventor of sin, the devil, talked Adam and Eve into doing the same. That's how sin entered our world, causing Adam and Eve's children and grandchildren to also choose sinful rule breaking. All this happened because God was kind enough to give us a choice of whether or not to love and obey Him."

"That's awful!" said Marie, "After giving them the whole world, God must have been really disappointed in people."

"Yes," said the King, "He was disappointed, especially since He knew sin would bring unfairness into people's lives and cause horrible things to happen in the world. But even after what they did, God still loved Adam and Eve, just as He continues loving every person He created. He wants to one day live with all His people, but the worst problem with sin is that sinners can't go to heaven. God is perfect love and truth, so He cannot be around sin."

Marie jumped up and said, "Yay! I'm going to heaven. I'm almost always good, and I love people."

Smiling, the king said, "Marie, let me ask you an important question: Are you a *perfectly* good person—like God? He gave us the Ten Commandments, which I am sure you girls know. Have you *ever* broken those rules? Even once?"

Marie thought about it and said, "I've never told any really bad, hurtful, terrible lies."

The king asked, "Marie, do you think our perfect God—who has never lied—only counts some lies and not others?"

Meanwhile, Rebecca was also thinking about the question. *I know Abby and I have lied. And I was with Marie when she lied to Princess Mirra. It was the day we met on the street after leaving the hospital. Rather than admit we got muddy in the dreadful forest, Marie told her it was just from playing.*

"Yes," said Marie. "I have lied."

"Thank you for being honest," said the king. "Anyone claiming they have not lied … is lying. Now, young ladies, what do you call someone who lies?

"Umm …," said Marie, "a liar?"

"Yes," said the king, "every person who ever lived has committed the sin of lying, so we are all sinners, just like our ancestors Adam and Eve."

With a suddenly sad face, Rebecca looked at the ground and thought about all her sins. Then the king asked her a question, "Miss

Rebecca, have you ever stolen anything … a toy, a piece of food, or even someone's place in line?"

Rebecca nodded, recalling the scissors she had taken from an adult's desk at the orphanage—and then lost them.

The king asked, "And what do we call someone who steals?"

"Bad," said Abby.

Rebecca said, "A thief."

The king's face turned quite serious. He said, "Now, I am not judging you girls. That's for God. He's a loving ruler, but He is also perfectly fair, meaning He cannot allow disobedience to go unpunished. As I mentioned, He can't let sinners into heaven, so when a sinner dies, the punishment has to be eternal separation from God, and the only other place to go is to live with the devil and other evil-doers.

Rebecca hung her head in despair, thinking, *There is no way God can let me into heaven. It wouldn't be fair.*

Marie said, "But if everyone disobeys God and no one gets to go to heaven, why are you and Princess Mirra so happy?"

The King smiled, "Excellent question, Miss Marie." Then he turned to his daughter and said, "Mirra, would you like to explain this to our guests?"

The princess looked at the girls and said, "That's the great news. Despite our sins, God wants us all to choose to live with Him in heaven, so He sent part of Himself to Earth in the form of a man named Jesus Christ. God put baby Jesus into His mother, Mary, and she gave birth to Him. He grew up like you and me as a human, but He was also fully God. Christ lived over thirty years and never broke God's rules. He didn't sin. Not even once."

Marie said, "Yes, because He was part of God, right?"

"Well," said Mirra, "He was also fully human, so like everyone else, He experienced the same temptations to sin. In fact, it was much worse for Him. When Jesus was the weakest of His entire life—having not eaten for forty days—the devil showed up in person to tempt Him. Satan offered Christ the whole world if He would just sin once. Jesus said no."

"He was a great man," said Marie, "I'm sure He's in heaven, right?"

Mirra continued, "Jesus Christ could have lived a long life and then gone to heaven because He's the only person who ever earned it. He broke no rules, committed no sin, deserved no punishment. Instead, He volunteered to do something wonderful for all of humankind, an act of love that was completely unfair to Him and brought Him the worst kind of pain and suffering.

"Jesus chose to sacrifice His life by *taking the punishment for the sins of everyone in the world.* In fact, before dying, He was beaten and whipped, and then forced to carry a heavy cross for miles. He was nailed to that cross and left to hang there for hours and hours, dying in one of the most painful ways possible.

"Jesus took the full punishment you and I deserved. But by doing so, He gave us the gift of forgiveness for all our sins, past, present, and future. However, we must choose to accept the gift if we want to go to heaven—as your parents did while they were still living."

Rebecca said, "But it's not right that Jesus did nothing wrong and He's dead, yet He made a way for us rule-breaking sinners to go to heaven."

"That's true," said Mirra. "But after three days of being dead, God brought Him back to life, took Him up to heaven, and gave Him a throne next to God."

"That's wonderful," said Rebecca.

"Thank you for that excellent explanation, Mirra," said the king.

King Mesharet turned to the orphans, "Like me, Queen Narissa, Princess Mirra, and apparently your parents, you young ladies have the choice to accept Jesus's free gift of forgiveness … or not. All you need to do is—"

"I'LL DO IT!" shouted Marie.

"ME TOO!" yelled Abby.

"Not so fast, you two," said the king, "You can only answer after you know the full question and what is expected if you say yes. The question is whether you believe Jesus died to take *your* punishment for *your* sins. And, if so, will you accept God's forgiveness made available by Christ's suffering and death? Then, if you say yes, God expects you to share the good news with others about what Jesus did. God wants everyone to hear about Jesus and choose heaven."

"So, Miss Marie Rose McKenna, to be a real princess under the King of kings, you must say with your mouth that Jesus is Lord and believe with your heart that God raised Jesus from the dead. Think hard. Get in touch with your heart and the decision is completely your choice. Now, feel free to say whatever you believe."

Uncharacteristically, Marie paused for a few moments and then calmly said, "I do say Jesus died for my sins. He is my Lord. I believe in my heart that God raised Him from the dead. Today Jesus sits in heaven with God—which is where I want to go one day. I want to be with my heavenly family, who will never, ever leave me."

"Well done, *Princess* Marie!" said the king. "You are a follower of Christ—a Christian. Welcome to God's royal family. He now sees you as sinless, like Christ. And no one and nothing can ever change that, not even you. For all eternity you *will* help Jesus rule creation under your Heavenly Father, the King of all kings.

Marie received joyful congratulations from Abby, Rebecca, and Princess Mirra. Then the king addressed the sisters, "Rebecca Findley Faith and Abigail Constance Faith, what say you?"

Abby shouted, "YES! YES!"

With a serious look on her face, Rebecca turned to her sister, "Abby, do you believe you have broken God's rules by telling a lie?"

"Yes, Becky," said Abby, "And I took things of yours, and I'm sorry."

Rebecca continued, "Abby, do you believe Jesus Christ died to take your punishment for breaking God's rules and that God brought Jesus back to life and took Him to heaven?"

"Yes," said Abby.

The king asked, "Well then, Miss Abigail, in your own words, please explain exactly what you believe?"

"God turned into baby Jesus," said Abby, "and He came to live with people. He was so good growing up that He never did anything bad. But then He allowed himself to be punished and die because of the bad things other people do. Now Jesus is in heaven, He's my Lord, AND I'M GOD'S PWINCESS!"

"Congratulations, *Princess* Abigail!" said the King. "Welcome to the royal family of God. As a follower of Christ, you are forever a Christian. No one can ever take that away from you, no matter what you do. You will be in heaven one day, as a sister-princess of Jesus, the Prince of the universe. Jesus is part of God, so He holds the highest position in creation—the Lord over everything."

The king looked at Rebecca and said, "Miss Rebecca Findley Faith, I have already heard your heart as you spoke to your sister, but what would you like to say?"

Rebecca said, "King Mesharet, I have broken God's laws and I deserve to be punished, but instead, I will accept His forgiveness through the sacrifice of God's only son, Jesus. Our Heavenly Father allowed Jesus to volunteer for a horrible death on a cross, even though He lived a perfect life and did not deserve it.

"But I did deserve the punishment He took for me. I am thankful Christ died for my sins, so I could still go to heaven to be with God, my Creator. I certainly don't deserve it, but I accept the gift. Jesus is Lord."

"YAY!" said Abby, jumping into her sister's arms.

Marie and Mirra joined in the hugs, and then even the King left his throne to congratulate the girls. He looked at Rebecca, and said, "Welcome *Princess* Rebecca to the royal family of God, Creator and Ruler of everything—the King of kings."

King Mesharet moved back to his throne and Princess Mirra took another turn at teaching the new princesses some biblical truth,

"If it's true that your mothers and fathers were Christians, then your parents had God's royal blood, just like what runs through your veins now that you've each accepted God's forgiveness.

"Unlike earthly royals, being a child of the King of kings means you can never lose your kingdom and crown, forever and ever, even after this life is over. After leaving this world, you will forever walk and talk with the Creator of the heavens and earth. *Today*, God sees you as His princesses."

All this information flooded Rebecca's mind. For the first time in her life, she felt an inner warmth that filled the hole of sadness she had always carried, the same hole that had grown much bigger when her parents died. Suddenly, she felt overwhelming joy, not just pleasure from something like cake, but joyful love for God, her own life, and the lives of everyone else God created.

With that same joy on all the girls' faces, the king said, "Princesses Rebecca, Marie, and Abigail, what is so wonderful about being a Christian is that the world only offers made-up stories of supposedly magical lands where only a few people ever get to live royal, enchanted lives. But because you princesses chose Jesus, the Bible says all of heaven is rejoicing—right now."

After the girls celebrated, Mirra added, "Princesses, the third and last part of God is the Holy Spirit. The day we accept Jesus's gift of forgiveness for our sins, God sends His Holy Spirit to live inside every Christian. Besides God the Heavenly Father and His Son Jesus being with you always, the Holy Spirit actually lives inside you to guide you through life."

"Mr. King," said Abby, "if I promise not to eat much, will God have enough room in my tummy?"

Everyone laughed, and the king said, "Princess Abigail, just like God, the Holy Spirit is a spirit who can be anywhere and everywhere, all at the same time, no matter how small the child."

Listening to the king's wisdom, Rebecca felt like she was at complete peace for the first time in her life. She thought, *I love my own earthly father and mother. I can't wait to see them again, but now I also have my Father God, Who will always love me and never leave Abby and me.*

Realizing she could silently thank God, Rebecca also whispered a short prayer to herself, "Father, thank you for saving me. I can't wait to see you someday in heaven. When I get there, can you please show me around and also take me to see a couple of stars? And don't worry, I'll explain things to Abby so she will understand everything about you. Also, God, you'll want to have Marie along—she's a lot of fun."

13

Home

Over and over, the new princesses thanked King Mesharet and Princess Mirra. Then all four girls spent the afternoon exploring the castle and riding horses through town, around the hills and meadows, near streams, and even in a forest.

They had many more questions for their sister-princess Mirra, especially about how their lives might change now that they were royal followers of the King of kings. At some point they went back to the castle for a delicious, late lunch. That was when Mirra surprised them with another life-changing offer from the king. "Princesses," she said, "King Mesharet asked if you girls would like to live here, either with us at the castle, or with a wonderful family in town."

"Yuuuh!" said Marie, through a mouthful of soup.

"I'll take that as a yes," said Mirra.

"Yes, yes, yes!" said Abby.

"Ye—" Rebecca was about to agree, but then began thinking about Jesus and the sinful world. She thought, *What would Christ do if He were me?*

"Rebecca?" said Mirra, "Don't you want to live here with us? We can explore, ride horses, swim, and eat wonderful food every day."

Rebecca spent a few more moments thinking, and then made her decision, "Princess Mirra," she said, "I thank you and the king for your generosity and kindness. Living here with you would be a fairy tale come true … but there's the problem. We weren't the only children suffering at the slum dump … I mean, orphanage. Like the other children still living there, just a couple days ago, we had little hope. Knowing that, I think Jesus would want us to help them.

"As God's princesses, we are asked to think about others more than ourselves, just like Jesus did. His whole life was about helping others get to heaven. And as a princess, you could have stayed near this amazing town and castle, just enjoying your wonderful life. Instead, you take long, bumpy rides to visit orphanages. Today your efforts caused a celebration in heaven. So, if Abby agrees, I think there's a way she and I can return your favor—and God's amazing gift—by going back to our … umm … home."

Mirra replied, "Princess Rebecca, you are brave. I can't think of a better way for you to thank Jesus."

"What about me?" said Marie.

Rebecca smiled and said, "Marie, we'll miss you terribly, but you and Princess Mirra will make a great team."

"No," said Marie, "I love Mirra, but we have much to do at the dump. Those little sinners aren't going know what hit 'em."

"YEAH!" said Rebecca.

"YAH!" said Abby, caught up in the excitement. But then the tiny girl's face turned sad, "Princess Mirra, can we come visit you again?"

"Of course, Abby," said Mirra. "You girls are welcome whenever you'd like. Even if I'm away, Queen Narissa is usually here. You three will love her. And Princess Abigail, though you can't do this often, when you really want to come see us, I'll give you a castle flag to put out on the road. During kingdom travels by servants, workers, and myself, one of us will surely see it soon, and we'll know you want to come visit. But Abby, promise you will always try to bring a *new* friend—or two."

"I will," said Abby. "And then you can tell them about God and how He loves us so much."

That evening the king put on a royal banquet in the castle's great hall in celebration of the new princesses. At the start of the meal, King Mesharet quieted the huge crowd and had everyone raise a glass for his royal toast, "We gather to rejoice over God's growing family. Today, thanks to my daughter Mirra, Princess Marie, Princess Rebecca, and Princess Abigail put their trust in Jesus. Tonight, we join heaven in celebration."

The crowd full of Christians cheered. After many hours of eating, dancing, singing, and other merrymaking, it was time for the girls to depart in Mirra's carriage. And Princess Mirra personally packed a travel basket for their journey.

King Mesharet handed Rebecca a letter with his royal seal. "Give this to the new headmistress," he said. "It will allow you girls the run of the building—within reason. This will help you each fulfill your desire to share the good news about Christ's gift of forgiveness and a peaceful and joyful life, followed by an even better eternity. But remember, your job is not to change hearts—the Holy Spirit will work on that. You need only tell them the truth that they may not already know. So, Your Royal Highnesses, go help give out some heavenly crowns.

One by one, *the peasant princesses* climbed up the stairs and took their seats inside the carriage. Princess Mirra followed, but then stopped at the top step and said, "I know you three will spread joy to the orphans. You are each volunteering for an important mission, so every night before I fall asleep, I will do my part and pray for your success. I look forward to seeing how your years with God will change you into wonderful, wise young ladies."

Princess Mirra gave them each a last hug and then stepped down, allowing their deer-drawn ride to pull out onto the road. After waving goodbye until they could no longer see Mirra, the newly Christian girls began talking about their plans to help others at the orphanage.

Eventually the subject turned to the old, familiar topic of kings, kingdoms, knights, realms, and quests. But this time, rather than Rebecca wishing for a prince to show up and take her and Abby away to his kingdom, Rebecca said, "When we get to heaven one day, would you two rather explore there first, or see some planets and stars? Or will we want to spend most of our time asking God questions?"

Abby said, "I just hope there's ice cweam."

After the long, exciting day, the princesses soon drifted off to sleep. Hours later, Rebecca rolled over and woke up when her head bumped something hard. Reaching back under a pillow, she pulled out a book that she held up to the candlelight. It was a Bible. She sat up quickly. "My very own Bible!" she said out loud. "Just as the king promised." Tears filled her eyes as she opened the pages, "I will never receive a more precious treasure." She sat and read in the dim light, starting with the first chapter, first page, and first sentence, "In the beginning, God made the heavens and the earth."

The heavens? There's more than one? I need to learn about that.

In a while, after Marie and Abby woke, they all had fun finding the other two Bibles. Then the older girls read to Abby until she fell back asleep, after which Marie and Rebecca took turns reading to each other. Rebecca loved the stories and knew right then that she would continue reading the Bible for the rest of her life—even though some of it was confusing at first.

After the long journey, they arrived at the orphanage, where the coachmen and outriders dropped them off and bid the princesses farewell. The girls thanked them and waved goodbye as the mighty stags pulled the carriage out of sight.

When the girls turned to go inside, Rebecca saw all the wide-eyed children staring out the windows, no doubt wondering who had been fortunate enough to have ridden in the royal carriage.

Looking at their faces, Rebecca's heart filled with joy to think about the young lives that would be changed. She thought, *Those children won't live in earthly castles, and terrible things will still happen to them, but I'm excited to tell them about how the Lord can take away some of their sadness during these difficult times. They might not get earthly parents before growing up, but right away they can choose to follow their Father in heaven. Their Creator wants to adopt them forever, if only they will be willing to follow Him.*

In just the first few months that followed, the girls were able to tell more than half the orphans about Jesus. Marie even gave the good news to some of the adults. The princesses continued reading their Bibles daily, learning more and more about the mind of God, and the exact purposes for which He made them, one of which was to be in a close, loving relationship with Him.

With the other children, the three girls began by sharing biblical truths—as the king and Mirra had done for them. Later they learned how Jesus had done the same with His twelve disciples, and then those men taught their own disciples. On and on the teaching and learning has gone, all the way up to today.

Each day, Rebecca grew closer to God, bringing her what the Bible promises to those who build a relationship with Him—greater and greater peace, love, joy, patience, kindness, goodness—and *faith*—like the sisters' last name.

When Rebecca first came across the word "faith" in the Bible, she thought, *I wonder if God gave us our parents because of their last name, knowing that Abby and I would one day put our* faith *in Jesus?* She decided He might have, because she'd learned that He knows everyone's future.

Rebecca still longed to see her mother and father again, but she felt she could wait as long as God wanted to keep her on earth, helping Him to lead princes and princesses into His kingdom. She would enjoy the wonderful reunion with her earthly parents someday, but she also knew she *really* only needed her Heavenly Father.

Many of the children at the orphanage prayed to accept God's love and gift of salvation, becoming princes and princesses in the family of God—the slum dump was never the same. Though some were not open to listen, and a few even became angry at the girls for mentioning God, they just kept planting seeds of *faith* and letting the Holy Spirit work on them. Over time, a place once filled with gloom and despair was being transformed into one with many contented and joyful children.

And it was because, as children and adults followed Jesus, they started focusing on others instead of themselves. This change led to happier people and a cleaner building. The adults began talking more with the orphans, and they even started serving better food.

Not long after they arrived back, while lying in bed one night, Marie had another adventurous idea, though it originally came from Rebecca the first day they met. While everyone in the building slept, Marie cracked open her door, and then crept along quietly in her stocking feet, down the hall and up the stairs to Rebecca and Abby's door.

After knocking quietly for about a minute, a sleepy Rebecca opened the door, and was only slightly surprised to see her princess friend. "Marie, what's the plan this time?"

"Wake Abby up. Both of you put on socks and come out. No shoes though. But wear two pairs of socks each, because yours have so many holes in them."

Ignoring the fact that Marie again wouldn't tell her the plan, Rebecca quickly dressed Abby and herself. They quietly followed Marie downstairs, into and through the deserted dining hall, and then out the back door. After they slowly closed the door to avoid any sound, Marie turned toward the playground and ran for some *empty* swings.

Suddenly Rebecca remembered. Her thoughtful friend was helping her fulfill the one ambitious adventure Rebecca had come up with during her two years there, sneaking outside while everyone else slept, allowing her and Abby to fly through the air together, each on her own swing.

For hours that night, the three friends swung, laughed, and talked. Rebecca was delighted to be alive, and even more excited about her future. She no longer saw herself as a peasant girl, for now she was a princess—the King of king's beloved daughter.

> *See what great love the Father has lavished on us,*
> *that we should be called children of God!*
> *And that is what we are! 1 John 3:1a (NIV)*

About the Author

Scott Bueling, along with his son Aiden, is the co-author of The Peasant Princess. What began as a father-son dream grew into a powerful story of faith, courage, and the pursuit of God's call. Scott brings years of leadership, mentoring, and storytelling experience, while Aiden's fresh perspective and imagination give the tale its heart. Together, they have crafted a story that blends adventure with timeless truth.

Their contributor, Michelle Cox, is an award-winning author with a decade of publishing experience with BroadStreet Publishing, Tyndale, David C Cook, and Post Hill Press. She is the co-author (with Brian Bird) of the bestselling When God Calls the Heart devotional series based on Hallmark Channel's #1 show, When Calls the Heart. Her upcoming titles include Divine Beauty: Becoming Beautiful Based on God's Truths, Send Me: Devotions to Inspire Your Heart to Service, and Our Daily Biscuit: Devotions with a Drawl (co-authored with Todd Starnes).

Together, Scott, Aiden, and Michelle have created a book that reflects both the innocence of a child's wonder and the wisdom of seasoned faith. Their goal is simple: to inspire readers of all ages to discover their God-given identity, rise above their circumstances, and live out the greater story they were created for.

Discover Scott beyond the pages—scan the QR code below for exclusive content, inspiring updates, and behind-the-scenes access!

9 781965 401606